"I figure we can negotiate the conjugal rights part, but I guarantee it wouldn't be a hardship on you."

"How romantic," Ann countered. "I can't recall the last time I had such a tender proposal."

"So that's why you haven't accepted any of them?"

Reed's remark was like a slap across her face. She'd never had a proposal.

"That's none of your damn business."

Reed ignored her as he juggled the baby and diaper bag. "Look at her, sugar. Hold her and then tell me you wouldn't do anything in the world to keep her if you were in my shoes."

He thrust the baby into Ann's arms.

Her emotions were like quicksilver as the infant snuggled close and rooted against her breast. Her heart ached, and she had difficulty drawing a breath. Stroking Betina's soft cap of hair, Ann looked at her through a veil of tears.

Was it possible that this time she could have it all? The hot sultry passion she'd felt so explosively when she was with Reed? And motherhood, too?

"H-how soon do you need to get married?"

ABOUT THE AUTHOR

Charlotte Maclay can't resist a happy ending. That's why she's had such fun writing more than twenty romance novels. Particularly well-known for her volunteer efforts in her hometown of Torrance, California, Charlotte believes you should make a difference in your community. She and her husband have two married daughters and two grandchildren, whom they are occasionally allowed to baby-sit. She loves to hear from readers and can be reached at: P.O. Box 505, Torrance, CA 90508.

Books by Charlotte Maclay

HARLEQUIN AMERICAN ROMANCE

474—THE VILLAIN'S LADY
488—A GHOSTLY AFFAIR
503—ELUSIVE TREASURE
532—MICHAEL'S MAGIC
537—THE KIDNAPPED BRIDE
566—HOW TO MARRY A MILLIONAIRE
585—THE COWBOY AND THE BELLY DANCER
620—THE BEWITCHING BACHELOR
643—WANTED: A DAD TO BRAG ABOUT
657—THE LITTLEST ANGEL
684—STEALING SAMANTHA
709—CATCHING A DADDY
728—A LITTLE BIT PREGNANT
743—THE HOG-TIED GROOM

Daddy's Little Cowgirl

CHARLOTTE MACLAY

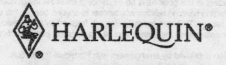

HARLEQUIN®

TORONTO • NEW YORK • LONDON
AMSTERDAM • PARIS • SYDNEY • HAMBURG
STOCKHOLM • ATHENS • TOKYO • MILAN • MADRID
PRAGUE • WARSAW • BUDAPEST • AUCKLAND

Special thanks to Anna Munro and Dan Patterson at The Soldier Factory in Cambria, California, for their warm welcome and detailed information.
Your exquisite miniatures inspired me.

ISBN 0-373-16766-0

DADDY'S LITTLE COWGIRL

Chapter One

Reed Drummond drove the thirty head of beef cattle down the narrow California blacktop highway. He could have used a partner to keep the animals in line. What he had was a mangy mutt.

He whistled, and the mutt nipped at the heels of the stragglers.

The winding road divided two main sections of the Rocking D Ranch, a thousand-acre spread located in the rolling hills that rose along the coastline of central California, not far from San Simeon and the Hearst castle. As Reed well knew, wherever you grazed cattle, the grass was always greener just down the road a piece. He'd traveled a lot of roads in his twenty-seven years, worked as a hired hand in a half-dozen different states and more than a dozen cattle ranches. Now he was back home again, had been for a month, and it sure as hell wasn't a castle.

Automatically he reached into his shirt pocket for his cigarette fixings and came up with a pacifier instead. He grinned.

Who would have thought he'd be a father, not to his own kid but to a brown-eyed sweetheart born to a young couple who'd latched on to him like Reed was their big brother or something. Until Betsy and Tommy had come along, he'd been a loner, a rolling stone that gathered no moss. They'd darn near adopted *him*, sticking like glue as they moved from ranch to ranch with him.

Maybe they'd stuck to him because they were runaways like Reed had once been—and with the same good reasons.

Those two kids were so tickled when Betsy got pregnant, too young to know better.

And then came the accident, Tommy driving their old jalopy, Betsy in the passenger seat, Reed a half-mile behind them in his pickup, all driving toward Fort Worth and a new job. Betsy made it to the hospital—barely. Tommy hadn't gotten that far.

Reed's throat closed on the memory, and he stuffed the pacifier back into his pocket. Betsy's very last request was that Reed take her baby, adopt little Betina and be the best daddy he could be.

He hadn't wanted to be responsible for a kid. A thousand other guys would have been a better choice. But Betsy had chosen him and with practically her last breath told him Tommy would have wanted it that way too. No way could he have told them no.

So he'd given up cigarettes cold turkey, hired a housekeeper, packed up Betina and brought her home to the Rocking D. He hadn't thought of his father's run-down cattle ranch as *home* in more than a dozen years. But he couldn't raise Betina on the road, living in bunkhouses wherever they happened to need a hired hand. That was no life for a kid.

The ranch had been his for more than two years, since his old man's liver had finally given out on him.

Betina needed a place to grow up, a place she could call home. Reed would damn well see she got it.

He'd given his word to her mother. It was that simple—and that complicated. Reed never went back on his word. Never.

"Keep on movin'," he urged the lead steer. "We haven't got all day."

The longer the herd was on the road, the greater the chances some tourist would come barreling through this scenic route at two hundred miles an hour and spook the cattle into a stampede. With only Reed and the mutt to control the animals, slowing a pack of runaway beef on the hoof would be a damn hard trick to pull off.

There was a school between this particular spot on the road and the pasture where Reed was heading. Nobody had ever bothered to put up a fence there, certainly not his old man, who'd spent more time drunk than sober.

For a moment, he smiled and thought about Betina—Bets, he'd taken to calling her—someday going to that same school. Good God! he laughed. He'd have to join the PTA! Wouldn't that just make the town mothers roll their eyes.

FIRE DRILL!

The shrill buzzer bleated repeatedly, echoing in the classroom and down the hallways, setting Ann Forrester's teeth on edge. To compound an already difficult week, the school principal had added one more distraction for the youngsters. She wondered how he expected her to get any teaching done at all between short days for parent conferences, student assemblies and now a fire drill.

"All right, students. Hand your test papers to me as you go out. And remember to stay in line all the way to the goalposts on the football field," she admonished the class of seventh-graders.

"I didn't get to finish, Miss Forrester," Rosetta complained, the ever-conscientious student.

"It's all right. We'll work on it tomorrow."

"Aw, gee, Miss Forrester." Jason handed her a paper so wrinkled it looked as if he'd had it stuffed in his pocket. Which, knowing Jason, he probably had. "I'm not gonna be here tomorrow. I've got a dentist appointment." He grinned.

"Then I guess you'll have to come by this afternoon after school to complete your test."

His smile crumpled. "Hey, no way, man. You're not givin' me detention just 'cause of some stupid—"

"Outside, Jason. On the football field," she ordered, trying to break up the logjam of students leaving the classroom. In a gesture of frustration, she flipped the ends of her long hair back behind her shoulder.

Preadolescents were at their most creative when

making up excuses not to do their work. Ann didn't let them get away with much, particularly a youngster like Jason. He had a great deal of potential but so far he'd wasted it all. Given that he was in foster care and had a terrible background of abuse and abandonment, it was little wonder he was a troubled child.

Her biggest weakness as a teacher had always been worrying about the kids who were at risk of being lost in the system. Bad boys invariably touched her heart the most. More times than not, her efforts to "save" them were a flop. Why she kept on trying was beyond her. It seemed a part of her nature she simply couldn't change.

With minimum organization, the students milled around the football field. Teachers tried to keep them contained, everyone waiting with equal impatience for Mr. Dunlap to give the all-clear signal.

Beneath her feet Ann felt a rumbling sensation. The ground quivered like Jell-O. What were the kids doing now? she wondered. Or was it an earthquake? She looked around for an explanation.

Suddenly her eyes widened in horror.

A cloud of billowing dust was rolling toward the unprotected students on the football field. The earth shook harder. The incessant roar increased.

"Stampede!" she screamed. "Run!"

Acting on instinct, afraid her students would be trampled—the kids she loved and worried over and cried for—Ann yanked off her sweater and waved it wildly in the air to divert the lead animals onto a new path.

"Get away!" she shouted. "Shoo! You don't belong here."

The smell of dust filled her nostrils; thundering hooves pounded closer as the herd veered away from the students—and directly toward Ann. She could see the lead animals, white blazes on their faces. Eyes wide. Heads bent with determination.

"No!" she screamed.

From out of nowhere, a horse and rider appeared. He bore down on her like an avenging angel. Sorrel horse. Stetson clamped low on the rider's head. Chaps flying. Heels flailing the animal's belly. Ann had a fleeting thought that if the cattle didn't kill her, this deranged cowboy would.

Without the horse missing a single stride, the rider lifted Ann off her feet, swung her up in front of him, and slammed her across his rock-hard thighs like a sack of flour. Every cubic centimeter of breath was driven from her lungs.

"Hang on, lady," he ordered.

As if she had a choice, she mentally muttered, grasping for whatever she could hold on to. The galloping pace threw her against the man's pelvis again and again. The ridge of the saddle horn dug into her midsection. Knee-high grass raced by in a blur at what seemed like only inches from her face. On her thigh, holding her, the cowboy's palm burned into her flesh.

If all the blood hadn't rushed to her head, she might have given serious thought to the position of her skirt, or wondered whether she'd donned a decent pair of panties that morning.

Before the worry of that embarrassment could take hold, the horse whirled, racing off in a new direction, paralleling the stampeding cattle, driving them away from the students who were scurrying for safety.

Finally slowing, the cowboy clamped his hands around her waist, twisting her, and righting her in his lap as if she were no more than a rag doll. Ann scrambled to restore some modesty to her skirt and drew her first full breath.

The scent of male and musk and leather invaded her senses along with the keen awareness of her rescuer's broad shoulders and muscular arms.

Oh, my...

He reined the horse to a stop, eased her to the ground and dropped down beside her, all in one fluid motion. The horse heaved a deep breath. Weak with relief, so did she.

"Lady, are you totally nuts or something?" Eyes the color of polished bronze glared at her. An angry glare. A look that mesmerized and made her mouth go dry. For a moment, Ann wasn't sure if she'd been rescued—or captured.

"Me?" she sputtered, trying to smooth her hair that was in wild disarray. "You're the one who was riding hell-bent for leather! You and your cows could have killed those children. I've never seen anything more dangerous, more irresponsible—"

"Didn't anybody ever tell you it's not real smart to wave a red flag in front of a bull?"

She blinked. "Those weren't bulls."

"Nope, don't suppose they were." He rested one

arm on the saddle and with his other hand thumbed his hat a little higher on his forehead. His lips curved ever so slightly as he perused her with a lazy, intimate glance. His gaze lingered overly long on her breasts, stripping her bare. "Still strikes me as a damn fool thing to do, though," he drawled.

Lord, he was a tall, slow-talking cowboy, his body lean and hard all over, his face tanned, his sideburns saddle-brown. Not pretty. Too rugged for that. Too insolent. And she shivered with suppressed pleasure at his too-familiar inspection of her. Lord knew how much more he'd seen of her while she'd been upended over his lap.

Glancing back toward the playing field, she saw the splash of red that used to be her sweater now trampled into the grass. "I guess I wasn't thinking. I mean, the children..."

"So you thought you'd plant your pretty little body right smack in the middle of their path and scare thirty head of rampaging beef cattle out of the way to protect those sweet little darlings. Now you tell me, sugar, who's the irresponsible one around here?"

Her pretty little body? Sugar? Ann didn't know whether to react to his unexpected comments or to the accusation that she was irresponsible. Why, she was probably the most responsible person she knew. With one devastating exception when she was seventeen years old, she'd *always* been reliable and dependable. The very nerve of this high-flying cowboy—

"Now, listen here, buster." She'd dealt with her

share of recalcitrant bad boys. This guy was no different, only older and a lot taller. And sexier. So sexy he was dangerous. "You're the one whose herd put those children at risk. If you hadn't let them stampede that way—"

His eyes narrowed threateningly, cutting her off, and squint lines appeared at the corners of those burnished eyes. "If some fool city slicker hadn't been driving the road too fast while I was moving my herd slow and peaceful-like, one of my steers wouldn't have gotten nicked by his car and the rest wouldn't have taken off at a dead run. And if you hadn't been waving that damn red flag, I might've turned the herd a mite sooner instead of having to pluck you outta harm's way." Idly, he stroked the sleek, sweat-dampened neck of his horse, his hand looking both big and gentle on the animal's rich, brown velvet coat. "For which you haven't yet thanked me, sugar."

"I, yes, of course, I appreciate—"

"You're welcome, sweetlin'." He touched the brim of his Stetson, a working hat stained by weather and sweat, not one a Saturday-night cowboy would wear out on the town. Nor were his jeans anything but practical, worn hard till they were nearly white and as soft as the warm leather gloving his thighs. His full lips twitched with the merest hint of a smile. "You're tough, teach. I'll give you that. Not many women would stand up to me...or to my cows like you did."

For one breathless moment, Ann wanted to bask in the glow of this stranger's compliment. She wanted to savor the feeling of being totally feminine against his raw, hard-edged maleness. But that was ridiculous.

She was a math teacher. Foolish notions about a tall, ruggedly handsome cowboy rescuing a damsel in distress had no place in her logical mind. Equations and orderly decimal points rested far more comfortably there.

Yet the scent of him did troubling things to her. His musky heat, the pungent aroma of maleness. Paralyzing things that threatened to consume her power to reason.

"Miss Forrester!"

Dragging her thoughts from the cowboy, she turned to the sound of Mr. Dunlap calling her name. The students were still milling around the football field—excited by the stampede—and the principal was jogging toward her across the grassy field beyond the playground. It occurred to Ann this was the first time she'd ever seen her principal move at a faster pace than a slow walk, and that with difficulty due to his ample girth. She hoped he wouldn't have a heart attack.

"Looks like you've been caught playing hooky, teach."

"Not exactly, but the children need to get back to class. So do I." To linger in this cowboy's company would be beyond foolhardy, not to mention a sure way to destroy her reputation in the small town of Mar del Oro.

"I'll give you a ride."

"No, that really isn't nec—" She squealed as he

grabbed her around the waist and hefted her up onto the back of the horse behind the saddle. Her full skirt bunched up to her thighs as she straddled the animal.

Then, in another fluid motion, one so graceful it was almost like a dance, he mounted in front of her.

Automatically she wrapped her arms around his waist to prevent herself from sliding off. With a shocking awareness, every feminine cell in her body registered the breadth of his back and the contour of hidden sinew and muscles beneath his shirt. "Don't you know how to take no for an answer?"

"Nope." He set the horse into an easy lope across the field. "Most times, when the ladies I know say no they really mean yes, or maybe. Thought I ought to give you the same chance, you being a high-class teacher 'n' all. Purdy as a little palomino filly I once had and just as sweet, I reckon. Wouldn't want you to miss out."

The man was incorrigible. In spite of that, Ann found herself smiling and wishing she could rest her cheek against the blue chambray fabric that covered his broad back. In the heat of the day, it would feel warm. And solid.

And she shouldn't even be considering such a thing.

They approached Mr. Dunlap, and the cowboy gave her his hand, helping her to slide off the horse. Ann looked up to thank him but he spoke before she had a chance.

"Of course, that filly I mentioned could be darn stubborn when she set her mind to it. A passionate little thing she was when she got riled.'' His bronze eyes twinkled with mischief as he spoke low and slow, his voice rusty and unfairly intimate. "She surely could keep a man on his toes, if you know what I mean. Reckon you could, too, sugar.''

Heat flamed her cheeks and the sharp thrill of excitement sped through her. She'd never had a man say anything so outrageous to her. Never. And she hated the way her heart lurched in her chest and the frisson of secret pleasure that swept through her midsection. That was no way for a woman to act. Particularly in front of her principal—even if he hadn't heard the cowboy's suggestive remarks.

"Miss Forrester, are you all right?'' Harry Dunlap asked between wheezing breaths.

"I'm fine. Really.'' Except for a mild case of heart palpitations, which she was sure would quickly pass. Though somewhere downstream she might have an erotic dream or two, this reckless cowboy playing a major role. She suspected he'd provide the hottest, most titillating—

"When you went running out to those beasts, we were all so frightened.''

"As you can see, this gentleman rescued me. No harm done.''

"Well, we certainly are grateful. The children…'' Tilting his head, Mr. Dunlap studied the cowboy. "Don't I know you, young man?''

"You've got a good memory, Mr. Dunlap. But then, I spent a hell of a lot of time in your office, didn't I?''

"Well, my sakes. Reed Drummond, isn't it?''

"One and the same." He touched the brim of his hat with a two-finger salute. "Nice seeing y'all again. Miss Forrester." With a nod, he wheeled the horse around and galloped off toward where his cattle were grazing peacefully. A shaggy black-and-white dog patrolled the perimeter of the herd, his tail wagging like a semaphore.

Mr. Dunlap pulled a handkerchief from his pocket and wiped his sweaty brow. "Oh, my, I'm not entirely pleased to see that young man back in town."

"Back?" she asked. "From where?"

"I heard he's been in Texas. A rolling stone, I suspect."

"Oh." That would explain his slow, cowboy drawl, she realized, her gaze following him. She noted how well he sat his horse, as if they had been molded together as one. He'd ride a woman the same way, she imagined. And the shock of that thought nearly made her knees buckle.

"He was a hellion as a youngster. Got into nothing but trouble all through junior high and high school. Never did graduate that I know of. Bad blood, I'd say. His father used to spend more Saturday nights in the jail than the police chief did. A fighting, brawling drunk, I heard."

"If his father was an alcoholic, maybe Reed had good reason for acting out." Unable to help herself, Ann had leapt to the cowboy's defense. Just as she would have if he'd been one of her students, she told herself. Except her feelings for him were far different than those she had for the adolescents in her classroom. *Far* different and quite unsettling.

They turned to walk back toward the school grounds. Mr. Dunlap was still a little breathless, and Ann kept their pace slow.

"I'm worried, now that that Drummond boy is back," Mr. Dunlap said. "His property adjoins the school's. If he can't keep his cattle in hand any better than he just demonstrated, we could be in for trouble."

"Maybe the school board ought to pay to put up a fence," Ann suggested. There were a lot of things the school board ought to be doing—like buying more and better books and additional computers, and hiring several more teachers in order to reduce class size. But they never managed to find enough dollars in their budget to make life easier for the teachers who worked in the trenches. Finding funds for a new car every year for the district superintendent didn't seem to be a problem, however. "Besides, Reed didn't exactly stampede the cows himself. A car spooked them."

"You assume a man like Drummond would respect our boundaries. I doubt he's changed much. He was always wild. He ran with a pack of boys back then. One night they broke out every single window at the elementary school. Of course he denied being involved. But we knew the truth. I tell you, people like Reed Drummond don't change."

A shiver slid down Ann's spine. If she had an Achilles' heel, it was for the kind of bad boy who'd tempted her in high school. That slip had cost her dearly. She'd spent years rebuilding her self-esteem. Deep in her heart, she still carried a sense of guilt for having been so gullible. And for having lost so much.

Not that Reed Drummond posed any real threat to her. In spite of his flagrant flirtation, he wouldn't really have any interest in a thirty-something who hadn't had a date in more years than she cared to remember. No doubt he could have any woman he wanted with a simple snap of his fingers.

She'd just as soon not count herself among his conquests. In fact, she'd make sure she wasn't.

SMOOTH FLANKS. A mane of golden-brown hair the color of the hills blushed by a late summer sunset. Eyes that held the hint of spring grass after the rains. A stubborn chin and lips so ripe, the urge to kiss them was a living, crawling thing in his belly.

Reed gave Fiero another stroke with the grooming brush but his mind was on the pretty little filly he'd met, not his favorite cow pony.

"Maybe if they'd had teachers who looked like Miss Forrester when I was in school I might've hung around longer." He grinned, remembering the principal had very clearly called her *Miss*. She hadn't been wearing any rings, either, on those soft hands of hers. Soft, smooth legs, too. Holding her across his lap, it had taken all his self-restraint not to slip his hand farther under her dress and squeeze the inviting swell of her butt. Gently. Over and over again until she was groaning and wanting more.

"What do you think, Fiero? Should I sign up for a little remedial instruction with that pretty little lady? Or should I plan to teach her a thing or two instead?'' Muscles tightened and heat stirred in his groin as he took the thought to its ultimate conclusion.

Ah, hell. He'd been without a woman too long or he wouldn't even be thinking like that. Why would a classy lady like Miss Forrester want anything to do with a high-school dropout who owned a ranch that was mortgaged to the hilt? A guy who'd saddled himself with raising somebody else's baby?

Still, any woman who was passionate enough— or crazy enough—to stand her ground in front of a stampeding herd of cattle ought be one hot mama in the sack. With the right man, that is.

Leaving Fiero in his stall, Reed tossed the grooming brush on the workbench. He rotated his shoulders as he walked out of the barn into the twilight that was settling over the rolling hills. From his vantage point, he watched the evening fog slip into the valleys of the coastal range and press against the hilltops like gray memories of the past.

The mutt followed him outside and parked himself on Reed's right foot. Idly, he stroked the dog's head.

Until his father died, he hadn't even considered coming home. Now it made sense. Little Bets needed a home. All things considered, this wasn't a bad place to grow up.

Glancing at the ranch house with its peeling paint and out-of-kilter porch, he clenched his fists. He was damn well going to prove he wasn't his father's son. He'd turn this run-down excuse for a cattle ranch into a paying proposition or break his back trying.

If not for himself, he'd do it for Bets. This would be her legacy. He'd make it a proud one.

He lifted his hat and ran his fingers through his sweat-dampened hair.

'Course, a man had a right to some curiosity now and again about a woman he met. He'd check around town when he had a chance. Somebody ought to know Miss Forrester's first name.

Not that calling her Sugar wouldn't suit him just fine.

He wasn't going to pursue the woman, though. For a man like Reed, Miss Forrester would mean nothing but trouble. He had plenty of that on his own.

Including a potential lawsuit if he didn't make sure his cows stayed in their own backyard.

There was a big ol' pile of fence posts out back of the barn and a couple of rolls of wire. Couldn't hurt to take a few precautions against another stampede, particularly in this day and age. He didn't exactly have a lot of insurance. And he damn well wasn't going to lose the ranch because of his father's negligence. Not when Bets's future was at stake.

Suddenly he was eager to go inside, to make sure he was there when the housekeeper he'd brought from Texas was ready to put Bets down for the night. Reed always fed her her evening bottle. The one in the middle of the night, too, for that matter.

He grinned. He was getting pretty damn good at changing diapers, too. When he had to.

He went into the house, tossed his hat on the

kitchen table and washed up. Lupe came into the room as he was finishing up.

"You're right on time, *señor*. Our little *chiquita*, she is getting hungry."

Reed took the baby and tucked her under his arm while Lupe got the bottle from the refrigerator. Bets nuzzled at his chest, rooting for some milk. "Hang on, sweet pea. You know I'm not equipped like your mom would have been. Your bottle's comin'."

He jiggled her gently, noting she still wasn't filling out the stretchy sleeper he'd bought when she was born, and the terry cloth flapped loosely like flippers on a seal. He'd had no idea how tiny a new baby could be.

She gazed up at him with her big brown eyes. A bubble of spittle formed on her bow-shaped lips. It popped, like she was giving him a raspberry, and she grinned as if she'd just accomplished the most marvelous thing in the world, telling off her old man.

He laughed, cuddling her closer. "Hey, there. How 'bout a little respect, huh?"

Taking the bottle Lupe had prepared, he went into the living room and sat down in the wooden rocking chair he'd bought at a flea market. A peace he'd never known existed settled over him as Bets took the bottle into her mouth, looking up at him with complete trust in her eyes.

He swore he'd move heaven and earth to make sure she never lost her faith in him.

JUGGLING HER KEYS and a briefcase full of papers to be graded, Ann walked up the steps to her house.

It was nearly dark. She was hungry and tired. Worse, she'd been edgy all day since her encounter with that herd of wild-eyed cattle and the dark-eyed cowboy.

Pretty little body, indeed!

At five foot six she hardly considered herself petite—except possibly to a man who had to be at least six foot two, every inch of which was solid muscle.

On the porch, she stooped to pick up a box that had been delivered. She tucked it under her arm, held open the screen with her hip and unlocked the front door.

The small two-bedroom house she called home was her pride and joy. Polished cherrywood furniture blended with pieces upholstered in subdued federal blue, reflecting her conservative taste and giving the living room a feeling of serenity. The kitchen featured a table in the same pleasant wood. That's where she dropped her armload.

The first thing she needed was a nice cup of tea to ease the tension from both her mind and her body. Then dinner and back to work grading papers.

She switched on the burner under the teakettle. As she waited for the water to boil, she studied the package that had arrived.

She smiled. She'd all but forgotten she'd ordered a miniature from Dora's Miniature World a week ago. Supporting local artists was a hobby of hers, although on a teacher's salary she couldn't do much. But over the years she had picked up a couple of nice watercolors and some small sculptures. Recently she'd been collecting a series of lead figurines that decorated her fireplace mantel.

Using a paring knife, she slit the tape on the white cardboard carton and discovered it was packed full of packing material. She dug her hands into it and pulled out a smaller box, spraying the plastic popcorn pieces all over the kitchen table in the process. The gold-embossed label read Dream Man Collection.

"Exactly what I need," she murmured. A four-and-a-half-inch dream man to take her mind off of one who was six foot two.

She lifted the lid and stared at the contents.

Carefully packed in molded foam, the lead figure rested on its side. Gingerly she lifted it from the box. And stopped.

This was definitely not the Dream Man she had ordered.

Instead of the image of a medieval knight with shield and lance, a miniature mounted cowboy rested in her palm. Heavy. Exquisite but not at all fragile. Painted in amazing detail, he was wearing a blue chambray shirt, fringed chaps and pale blue denim pants. The sorrel he rode glistened as though the acrylic paint had actually turned to sweat on the animal's chestnut neck and flanks.

"No," she whispered. "It's not possible."

With fingers that shook, she removed the dusty brown Stetson from the molded foam and placed it on the cowboy's head. It fit perfectly, so low on his forehead she could barely see his polished-bronze eyes.

"No," she said again, more loudly. Her empty stomach knotted and her mouth went dry. "This is definitely the *wrong* dream man for me."

Chapter Two

She set the miniature down on the table with great care and backed away, eyeing it in dismay.

There'd been some sort of mix-up. That was it. The postal system had been known to make mistakes, right? Of course they did. She'd even received a Christmas card in April once—mailed two holiday seasons earlier.

Feeling relieved that she'd applied some logic to an illogical situation, she shifted her hair behind her shoulder and drew a deep breath. Dora probably sold dozens of these lead figures. It was simply a bizarre coincidence that Ann had met Reed Drummond today. It didn't mean a thing that the miniature resembled the flesh-and-blood man.

In amazing detail.

She swallowed hard, her heart doing erratic things in her chest.

What she needed to do was get the miniature back to Dora. Exchange it. It was absolutely, positively all wrong for her. It would look entirely out of place on her mantel.

Her stomach went tight as the image of the live cowboy popped into her mind—looking perfect in her bed.

The phone rang, startling Ann almost out of her skin.

Picking up the wall phone, she said, "Hel-lo." Her voice cracked.

"Ann, dear, are you all right?"

She cleared her throat. "I'm fine, Mother."

"I called earlier and you weren't home."

"I worked late."

"You do that too much, dear. You need to get out more. Have a little fun."

Ann repressed the sigh that threatened to escape. "Yes, Mother." In spite of herself, her gaze caressed the cowboy miniature. What a woman could do with a full-size man like that! And what he'd very likely do with her.

"I just wanted to make sure you'll be joining us for dinner Wednesday night."

With a jerk of her head, she glanced away from the cowboy. Neither of her parents would approve of Reed Drummond—or even a miniature of such a character placed on her mantel. They'd be more appalled at the prospect of him alive and in her bed. "Of course, Mother. That's our night out together."

For as long as Ann could remember, the Forrester family had gone out for Wednesday-night dinner. In a tourist town you picked the least busy evening of the week to eat out. It had become a ritual, one Ann found both comfortable and somehow boring. In contrast, her mother seemed to thrive on being queen bee for one night a week. Ann could hardly blame her. As the wife of the local bank president—now emeritus—her life had been pretty well constricted.

Her parents had wanted Ann's existence to be equally circumspect. In a rare act of foolish rebellion, she'd failed them once. And paid a terrible price.

"That's good, dear. Your father has invited the new bank manager to join us."

"Fine," she responded, barely listening to her mother. Instead she was thinking how totally *uncircumspect* it would be if she had an affair with a cowboy like Reed Drummond. The mere thought brought a shiver of forbidden excitement, and she closed her eyes against the sensation. "Mom, I'm really tired. I've got to fix myself something to eat."

"Of course, dear." Her mother rattled on for a minute or two more about the Mozart concert they were planning to attend in San Luis Obispo, the nearest town of any size, about forty minutes away.

When Ann was finally allowed to hang up, she did so with a deep sense of relief. She sat down at the kitchen table and stared at the cowboy figurine. He'd probably much prefer Texas two-stepping over a sonata any day of the week. Of course, sonatas were difficult to dance to, and Ann hadn't been dancing in a very long time.

"Oh, for heaven's sake!" Springing to her feet, she grabbed for the phone. Forget eating. She'd call Dora right now—

Except it was well past the store's closing time.

Even if she was a good friend, Ann could hardly intrude on Dora's private time simply because there had been a mix-up in the shipments. It wasn't a major crisis. Tomorrow after school would be soon enough to return the miniature and pick up a proper dream man of her own.

"MISS FORRESTER! That cowboy's back."

Ann whirled, nearly slamming her briefcase into the youngster who'd made the announcement. The keys she'd been holding dropped to the ground in front of her classroom door, the one she'd been about to unlock. Another student bent to pick them up.

"The cowboy?" Her throat was so tight, the question came out in a squeak.

Jason swaggered into the group of children who were clustered around her door. "Bet he's got the hots for you, Miss Forrester."

She glared at Jason. "I thought you had a dentist's appointment today."

He shrugged, his grin not in the least contrite for either his lie of yesterday or his comment of the moment.

Marcy McCullough, one of Ann's fellow teachers joined the gathering. "The kids are right. That cowboy is out on the playing field. Digging holes, as near as I can tell. You're going to have to take care of it."

"Me?" She nearly choked. "What holes? Can't Mr. Dunlap—"

"He's at some training institute in Santa Barbara

today. It's your turn in the barrel as assistant principal.''

"Oh, swell. Can't someone else talk to him? I haven't even opened up my classroom yet." And the very last person she wanted to see this morning was Reed Drummond. One restless night with images of him interfering with her sleep was more than enough.

Looking vaguely amused, Marcy said, "I'm sure you're the best one to handle the situation. I'll watch your class while you find out what's going on."

She gnashed her teeth. "Thank you. I'd appreciate that." In no mood for fun and games, Ann snatched the keys from the student who had picked them up and unlocked the door. She marched inside, dropped her briefcase on the desk and strode back outside. The small crowd of students parted for her. "Anybody who messes around while Mrs. McCullough is in charge can figure on a week's worth of detention. Got that, kids?"

"Oooo-eee," Jason chortled. "The new principal's one mean lady. You're scaring us, Miss Forrester."

If Jason wasn't so darn cute, in an arrogant adolescent way, Ann would have belted him. Except she'd never really think of striking a child. And she had a much taller, though equally arrogant male on her mind.

A man who wasn't wearing a shirt, she discovered when she reached the football field. Half the pubescent girls in the school had made the same discovery. They were lingering coyly in clusters of threes and fours around the perimeter of the mowed field. Drooling, Ann suspected, while Reed worked in the empty field of wild grass beyond the developed area—off-limits to the students.

"All right, girls. The first bell's going to ring any minute. On your way..."

"Aw, Miss Forrester..." several girls complained in unison.

Ignoring them, she angled through the tall grass directly toward Reed Drummond. Even though it was early morning and the air cool, his back glistened with sweat, accenting the flex of muscle and sinew as he worked. He didn't have a horse today. Instead an old pickup truck with a gun rack across the back window was parked in the field nearby.

"Just what do you think you're doing?" she asked.

Slowly, he lifted his head. A smile teased at the corners of his lips as he touched his fingertips to brim of his Stetson. "Good mornin' to you, too, sugar."

A giddy feeling as though she'd gotten too much sun swept over her. Lord, he had a nice chest. Not too much hair, just a few soft swirls that clung damply to his chest and arrowed downward toward—

She shook the thought from her mind. "I asked what you're up to."

"I'm building a fence." He leaned lazily on what she now realized was a posthole digger, not a shovel.

"On school property?" she asked, astounded.

"Nope. This here is Rocking D land. The mile post on the highway and that old oak down in the gully mark the boundary."

She followed his gaze toward a gnarled tree about five hundred feet away. "This is your property?" Mr. Dunlap had said the school adjoined Drummond's land but she hadn't realized quite how close a neighbor he was. Much too close in her view.

"Yep. Sure is. I don't figure my stock is likely to stampede again any time soon but I thought better safe than sorry. I had a few old posts and some wire lying around. Oughta be enough to keep my steer from wandering into the school yard. Wouldn't want any of the kids to get hurt."

"That's...wonderful." It would have taken years to get any sort of fencing included in the school district capital budget. Reed had simply found a few old posts lying around and gone to work. "Very thoughtful of you."

"That's me. I'm a real thoughtful guy."

"Yes, well...ah..." Normally she wasn't tongue-tied. But standing here talking with Reed, the green hills behind him like a glorious backdrop for his sculpted masculinity, Ann was having a whole lot of trouble thinking at all, much less putting an entire coherent sentence together. "I wonder if you could possibly put on your shirt." *Or, as an alternative, let me run my hands over your chest.*

"Does seeing me without a shirt bother you, sweetlin'?"

Heat flooded her cheeks. "No, of course not. It's

just that we have a lot of impressionable young girls—''

"And you find me impressive."

"No. I find you impossible."

He flashed a raffish grin that was meant to unsettle her. It did exactly that.

"Not me, sugar. I'm easy." Still smiling, he picked up his shirt from where he had tossed it casually on the ground and tugged it on. "Ask anybody."

She didn't need to ask. Reed Drummond was the kind of man who had a girl in every port—or in every rodeo town. He reeked with the knowledge that women swooned at his feet with the least provocation. And provocative was his middle name. In capital letters.

Ann Forrester wasn't going to fall for his slick line. Not in this lifetime.

As soon as she could after school, she was going to take that damn miniature back to Dora. She wanted all reminders of this man out of her life.

The bell rang for first period and she turned to go back to her classroom.

"You all have a nice day, you hear, sugar Ann?" Reed called after her.

She nearly stopped in her tracks. Only with the fortitude built upon years of self-discipline was she able to keep walking. He knew her name. And he'd given it a sugar coating like no man she'd ever known.

HE WAS OUT THERE all morning. In the break between sixth-grade remedial math and eighth-grade algebra, Ann spotted him. Working. His shirt damp with perspiration. The row of fence posts extending one by one.

By lunch he'd gathered a group of admirers around him, Tom Sawyer–style. The boys had been given shovels; the girls simply stood and watched in giggling admiration. His shirt had come off again.

In the teachers' room, it was obvious every female faculty member had noted—in precise detail— the circumference of Reed Drummond's biceps. They would have started a dollar-a-bet pool, but no one was courageous enough to volunteer to measure the man.

Ann had noticed other qualities, too. The tightness of his buns. The way he took off his hat from time to time and ploughed his fingers through thick, wavy hair. Achingly soft hair, from the way it tended to fall across his forehead.

She also observed how some of the boys were so hungry for male attention—Jason Hilary, in particular—that they had latched on to the cowboy. Shadowing him. She hadn't yet decided if that was a good idea or a bad one.

She did know she was grateful when the day ended. Tension of the magnitude she'd been experiencing did not make for a good learning environment. Gritting her teeth, she wondered how long it would take Reed to complete his fencing project.

A SOLID STRING of tourist cars edged along the main street of Mar del Oro, the drivers searching for an angled parking spot at the curb. With the warmth of California springtime, vacationers filled the coastal community, swarming through the craft shops and art galleries that lined the street. It would be worse when summer came.

Like most locals, Ann knew about back alleys and hidden parking spots reserved for business owners. She whipped her sporty Mustang into an unmarked slot behind Dora Peterson's van. Though Ann lived a quiet, circumscribed life, she rebelled at the thought of driving a boring car.

Tucking the Dream Man box under her arm, Ann entered Dora's Miniature World through the back door. Whole armies of lead figures were on display, from Napoleon's soldiers in full, colorful regalia to the blue and gray fighting the war between the states one more time, and British soldiers of World War I all set to do battle against the Huns. And in the other corner of the shop, pewter figures from Tolkien's *Lord of the Rings* looked ready to snarl and growl, dragons defending their lairs.

The miniatures were authentic, true works of art. Ann, steeped in teaching math to uninterested junior high school students, marveled at the artistic ability of the creators.

Busy with a customer, Dora waved from behind the counter. She and Ann had been in school together, and Dora had taken over the shop when her father had suffered a heart attack. She'd varied the merchandise, buying from outside sources as well as from the craftspeople in Mar del Oro and developing an extensive mail-order business. From all Ann could tell, Dora was a grand success.

Though mistakes in shipping did happen, Ann reminded herself.

Dora finally disengaged herself from her customer. "Hi, hon. Back for another Dream Man?"

"Not exactly." Ann placed the box on the counter. "I'm afraid there was a mix up in shipping."

Dora raised her eyebrows. A tall woman with sharp features, she'd never be considered pretty. But her heart was pure gold. "What's wrong?"

"I ordered a medieval knight. What I got was a cowboy." One with a striking resemblance to a cowboy who'd been inserting himself into her dreams lately.

"Cowboys aren't all bad," Dora commented with a grin. She lifted the lid on the box. "Say, what were you doing in San Luis Obispo last Wednesday?"

"Wednesday? Couldn't have been me. That was a school day, and I had dinner with my folks that evening." As usual.

"Funny," she said, eyeing Ann curiously. "I could have sworn it was you. I gave you a shout but you didn't turn around. Thought it was strange for you to be over there during the middle of the week."

"I deny everything. Teachers aren't allowed to play hooky." She laughed but her thoughts were on a tall cowboy who was sexy enough to lure any woman into skipping class. "You don't happen to know if, ah, the artist who made the cowboy figure uses local models, do you?'' Ann's question sounded as subtle as a sledgehammer slamming down on the glass countertop.

''I don't think she uses models at all. It'd be unusual for this kind of work.'' She glanced at the miniature. ''Why do you ask?''

''Oh, no reason. I just met this man—''

Dora's brows shot up again.

''No, nothing like that. I mean, there are some similarities. Nothing important. I thought, well, maybe—'' Maybe she was being a fool. And not for the first time, she thought, shifting her hair back behind her shoulder.

Shooting a glance toward a couple of new arrivals, Dora said, ''The artist just shipped me some new inventory. I haven't even opened the boxes yet. Maybe there's a knight in the batch. We can exchange—''

''That would be perfect. Sorry to be such a pest.''

''Not to worry.'' She reached across the counter and took Ann's hand. ''And as soon as I'm not so busy, I'll be dying to hear more about this *man* you met.''

''There's nothing to—'' But Dora wasn't listening. She'd gone off to help the customers, and before she had finished with them, a new group had come in the door. In between she retrieved several Dream Man boxes from the back room.

Ann checked through them, finding the medieval knight she'd wanted all along. That's when a gentleman who'd mistaken her for a store clerk asked a question. Since Ann knew the merchandise reasonably well, she put down her Dream Man box beside the others and showed the visitor to the cabinet featuring a diorama of Custer's Last Stand.

Leaving the elderly gentleman in Dora's capable hands, she escaped the store with her rightful Dream Man box.

Only then did she realize she'd left her briefcase at school, including all the papers she'd intended to correct that evening. By the time she returned to school, she was anxious and testy, ready for a fight, barely clinging to her usual calm demeanor.

Jason Hilary and his friends became her target the moment she saw them with cans of spray paint in their hands.

"Don't you try to run away," she shouted, piling out of her car and running after the boys. "I see you, Jason Hilary. Take one more step and you're dead meat."

"Aw, man..." He came to a halt while the rest of the boys sprinted away.

"Hand it over," she ordered.

"I didn't do nuthin'," he complained.

"Yeah, sure. A real saint." She snatched the can of black enamel from him.

Under his breath he muttered words no woman ought to hear or be subjected to.

"Jason, you're too smart to get yourself involved in something as stupid as painting on the walls. If you'd just settle down, your future—"

"Like, who the hell cares, Miss Forrester? Like, who gives a damn about what I do?"

She felt like she'd been slapped in the face. He

was right, of course. His parents, the whole system, had failed him. From his perspective there wasn't a soul in the world who gave a diddly damn about him.

Except her. She cared so much it hurt. The pain of his disillusionment lodged in her throat as painfully as if she'd swallowed one of those boulders that rolled down from the hills, blocking traffic and creating general chaos.

She had to do something for this boy before he was totally lost. But how could she? Few teachers, particularly female teachers, could reach such a troubled youngster. He needed someone stronger. Someone who'd been there. Someone who had survived.

In her mind's eye she suddenly pictured Reed Drummond. From what she'd gathered, he'd been around the same block Jason was traveling. A painful path. Surely he must have learned something that he could pass on to this young boy. *Something helpful.*

"I care about you, Jason." She cupped the boy's chin, forcing him to look her in the eye. The promise she was about to make terrified her, but she didn't see she had any choice. Jason's entire future was at risk. He was at a crossroads. She knew that from years of experience with children she'd rooted for and lost. She was damn well not going to lose Jason in the same way, if there was any chance to reclaim him. "And I think I know someone else who cares, too."

"Like who?" His gaze narrowed as though he

couldn't believe *anyone* would give a fig about him, much less two people.

"Promise me you'll be at school tomorrow."

He shrugged. "I was thinking about taking off. This place sucks."

"You can't leave. Where would you go?"

"My mom's in L.A. She'd take me back."

Right, just where Jason needed to be, with his drug-addicted mother who let her boyfriends beat the hell out of her son. "Los Angeles is two hundred miles away," she said, trying to discourage the boy. "You don't have any money. How are you going to—"

"I can hitchhike. Guys do."

"And some of them get killed," she reminded him. "Look, Jason, give me a chance. Maybe there's something I can do to help. A day or two. That's all I'm asking."

He glanced away. "I haven't done my homework yet."

Ann suppressed a smile. She'd won—for now. "Then I guess you'd better get your butt on home. I'm pretty tough when it comes to homework."

His rakish grin reminded Ann of the smile of another man, a reckless cowboy she'd have to turn into an instant mentor for a troubled boy.

Not for minute did she think she'd given herself an easy assignment.

Chapter Three

He heard her car drive up to the ranch house. From inside the barn, he watched as her tight skirt hiked up to her thighs when she got out. She looked around. Tentative. Interested.

The mountain coming to Mohammed.

Reed hadn't thought she would be this easy.

The mutt woofed and trotted out to meet her. As casually as if they were old friends, she knelt to pet the mangy dog. His tail wagged fiercely.

In spite of her showing up at his place, Ann Forrester had innocence written all over her. She used it as a shield to hide her passionate nature. Or maybe she wasn't aware of the appetites Reed sensed lurking right below the surface. Now that would be a honest-to-God shame, if she didn't know what she was missing.

A man could do a lot with a woman who looked at him the way Ann had that morning, those grass-green eyes speaking volumes about curiosity. And hunger. If she wasn't exactly willing right off, with a little coaxing it wouldn't take long. And she was here. So close he could feel the vibrations of her through the air.

He stepped out of the shadows into the long rays of the setting sun.

"Somethin' I can do for you, sugar?"

She let out a tiny gasp of surprise, the kind of sound a woman makes when a man first enters her—just before she moans at the sweet, hot pleasurable friction of him filling her all the way.

"Yes, yes, there is." She stood, and the mutt nuzzled her hand. "I, ah, hope I haven't caught you at a bad time." She looked uncertain now. Nervous.

"Just doing chores." He hooked his thumbs in his jeans, studying her. Letting her get a good look at him. Letting her decide. For now.

"I won't take much of your time." In a nervous gesture he'd seen her use before, she flicked her long hair back, revealing more of her smooth, kissable neck.

"I've never been a man to hurry things." Slow heat was better. Until it was a firestorm that couldn't be stopped. Then fast. And hard. And as long as possible.

Her high-heeled shoes were all wrong for walking on the uneven ground, her tight skirt too confining. She was too citified, too soft for ranch life.

Reed liked soft, and he hadn't had much of that in his life.

She stopped in front of him, her eyes locked on his. "You're sure I'm not disturbing you?" The tip of her tongue peeked out and swept a line of dampness across the fullness of her lower lip.

Reed felt the gesture right behind the snaps on his jeans. "You're doing a fine job of disturbing me, if that's what you're after."

"I mean...keeping you from your work."

"Most chores can wait...if there's a good reason." She'd be reason enough but Reed suspected she didn't know what she was asking for. Bedding her wouldn't be real smart. She might be hot between the sheets but she was dangerous, too. One of those "nice" women who confused making love with something else. Something permanent. They turned harpy when a man decided to move on down the road. Screaming mad. Or weepy.

Reed was almost surprised by his reluctance. Then again, no sense adding to the troubles he already had cluttering his life. And his responsibilities.

"How 'bout we compromise," he said. Lifting his hand, he fingered the tips of her golden-brown hair right where it lay against her throat. Silken threads turned to rose by the sun. His body complained bitterly that his good sense had taken over, denying him release from the tautness that was already building. "I'll keep on doing my chores and you can tell me what it is you want."

Torturing himself, he ran his thumb along the edge of her jaw. Warm, soft velvet.

Then he turned and walked into the barn.

Ann exhaled slowly. Unsteadily.

Definitely a bad idea, coming here. Reed was more man than she'd ever had to handle. The volatile chemistry between them—at least on her side— had an explosive quality, like kids playing with chemicals to make flash powder in the high school lab. The results could be blinding.

The aroma inside the barn was ripe and rich and earthy. Masculine. Nothing like what Ann was used to. No smell of old textbooks or copier ink. No feminine touch like a flower in a vase or a fake apple on the corner of the desk. This was real. Both unexpectedly riveting and bordering on dangerous.

Reed's horse was tied in the center of the barn. Silently, he lifted the animal's back hoof and began scraping the gunk out. Ann felt ill at ease. Out of her comfort zone, fighting the urge to flee. If it weren't for Jason, she'd do just that. The child was the reason she was here. No ulterior motive. She'd swear to that in a court of law, or so she told herself.

"What's your dog's name?" she asked, as much to hear her own voice as to put off asking for Reed's help. He could say no so easily, and she'd made a promise both to herself and the boy.

"He doesn't have a name."

"Of course he does. All pets have a name."

He looked up from his work. Beneath his hat she could barely see the glint of his bronze eyes in the fading light. "He's not a pet. He's a mutt and a working dog."

"But how do you call him when you want him to come?"

"I whistle. He knows what to do."

"That's cruel." She glanced at the dog in question, who'd plopped himself down nearby. His tail twitched. "Without a name, there's no dignity. Even for a dog."

Releasing his grip on the horse's leg, Reed straightened. "Lady, when you give an animal a name, then you begin to care about him. That's not a real good idea on a ranch. Animals die. A dog gets into a chicken coop and somebody shoots him. Or a horse steps in a hole, breaks his leg and has to be put down. Out here in the country it doesn't pay to get too attached."

Ann shuddered. What terrible losses Reed must have experienced to become so hardened against caring. Sympathy welled inside her, and she made a valiant attempt to quash the feeling. The effort wasn't entirely successful.

"Don't you name your horses either?"

He rested his hand on the sorrel's rump. "This one came with a name when I bought him. Fiero. He'd been in a stable fire and they were going to turn him into glue. I bought him cheap."

She sucked in a quick breath. He treated pain so casually, but he'd also rescued the animal from certain death. Reed was an enigma, a man she might never understand even if she spent a hundred years trying. Which, of course, she had no intention of doing. "Well, I think Arnold deserves a name, too."

He frowned. "Who's Arnold?"

"Your dog. Arnold's a very dignified name. He deserves it, don't you, boy?" His tail picked up speed and he stood, stretching.

"You're nuts."

"Come here, Arnold, honey." She smacked her lips together and held out her hand. "Let's show your master you know your—"

Reed whistled two short bursts, and the dog dropped to his belly. With angry strides, Reed closed the distance to Ann, moving purposefully into her personal space. "How 'bout we get to why you're here, sugar?"

She retreated a step and her back made contact with the rough wood of a stall. She lifted her chin. "I wanted to ask a favor of you."

"Just what sort of a favor would that be?"

His scent was as potent as the earthy aromas in the barn. Fully as masculine and totally arousing. Desperately she tried to ignore her instinctive reaction to him. Her erotic reaction. "One of the boys who was helping you with the fence posts today needs a male role model. Someone who could mentor him. I was hoping that you might consider—"

"Me?" The word erupted on a near laugh. "You've gotta be kidding, right?"

She bristled. "I never joke about my students."

"Then why the hell would you think—"

"Mr. Dunlap mentioned you weren't exactly a model student when you were in school, and that you'd run away when you were quite young. Jason is a troubled youngster. He needs to know someone cares about him before he throws his whole life away. I thought you'd be able to relate to him better than I can."

"Because you've never done anything wrong or stupid in your entire life."

The accusation stung because the opposite was the case. "That's not entirely true," she admitted.

His sculpted brows rose in a slow, suggestive motion. "Hard to believe, teach."

"What I may or may not have done in the past is not at issue here. It's Jason I'm worried about. What I'm asking of you is to spend some time with the boy. Talk to him. Let him know you care about what happens to him."

"And if I don't give a damn about the kid?"

"He has a name. It's Jason, and you will care if you give yourself—and him—a chance. He's in foster care. The family's fine but they've got six children to worry about. Jason needs to be special to someone, or I'm afraid he's going to go bad."

Reed braced his hands against the wall on either side of her, effectively trapping her between his arms, and brought his face so close she could feel the warmth of his breath on her cheeks. "You have a weakness for bad boys, huh?"

"Yes." Her throat closed tightly around the word. In Reed's eyes she saw flecks of gold hidden in the narrowing band of bronze. His lashes were unfairly long for a man; the slight hump on the bridge of his nose suggested it had been broken, at least once. Probably in a fight. His full lips tempted a woman to taste them, to explore their texture, their moist heat. Tempted her to want to be bad.

"If I did this little favor for you, teach, just what would be in it for me?" The low rasp of his question implied a simple thank-you would not be enough. The price would be far higher than that.

"I can't promise anything," she hedged, her heart

tripping uneasily in her chest. "Perhaps the school—"

"That's not what I'm talkin' about and you know it, sweetlin'."

Tilting his head, he leaned forward. It didn't take much before his lips slanted over hers, claiming her mouth with soft, warm, determined pressure. There was no escape. Though only their lips were touching, she was as helpless to move as if she'd been chained to him. She felt herself yielding. Giving way to urges she'd denied for years. Wanting. Craving. Hungry for the taste of his raw sensuality.

Even as she opened to him, fear trembled through her. How would she ever be able to stop? His tangy flavor was addictive, his potency irresistible. She needed to push him away. To refuse to travel a path that had once cost her so dearly. But even as she recognized the wisdom of that thought, her tongue tangled with his. Mating. Matching his every thrust and parry with one of her own.

Blood pulsed low in her body. Muscles clenched. Though the connection between them remained the same, his kiss touched her all over. Touched her clear to her soul.

A moan aching with need vibrated through her throat. At her sides, she tightened her fists into balls to prevent herself from linking her arms around his neck, from dragging him down to the ground with her where he could ease the terrible wanting that throbbed through her.

Changing the angle of attack, he sucked her lower lip between his teeth, holding her there in an impossibly gentle grip. She was his captive. His willing prisoner. A victim of her own weakness. More vulnerable than she had ever been in her life.

A sob rose and she jerked away, freed as easily as she had been captured. Her breathing came in ragged little pants. So did his, his eyes almost entirely black now as he held his position, their faces only inches apart.

She fought for the control she'd exercised so carefully over the years since her one rebellious slip. Struggled to find that strong inner core. She gathered herself.

"I trust you'll find that adequate payment," she said, proud that in spite of her thundering heart and trembling body, her voice was even.

"Not a chance, sweet sugar-Annie," he drawled. His lips curved ever so slightly. "I figure that was only the down payment."

Ann fled. There was no other way to describe her frantic escape.

In a breathless dash, she reached her car just as someone opened the front door to Reed's house. An older woman stepped out onto the porch, the light from the window slanting across her heavyset figure. In her arms she carried a baby.

Eyes wide, Ann froze at the open door to her car.

A baby? No one had mentioned Reed had a child. Dear heaven, did he also have a wife?

Revulsion churned in Ann's stomach and her entire being rebelled at the thought that she had just been thoroughly kissed by a married man. And she had enjoyed it.

She threw herself into the car, twisted the key, and slammed the car into gear. She *never* should have come here.

REED CHUCKLED as he watched gravel spray from under the tires of her Mustang and she sped down the farm road. Smart lady.

He thumbed his hat farther back on his head. She had no business hanging around with the likes of him.

He'd given her a good fright. Served her right, too, coming up here with her tempting body and those sweet, sultry lips of hers. Teasing a man. Giving him a helluva hard-on, which served him right, too.

Normally he didn't mess with "nice" women. But she'd gotten to him. Asking him, of all people, to worry about some predelinquent kid? When he hadn't been looking, somebody must have stamped Sucker on his forehead. It was the stupidest thing he'd ever heard.

About as dumb as naming an old mutt Arnold.

He look down at the dog, who'd parked himself right up against Reed's leg.

"Arnold."

Tail flagging, the dog leaned into him.

"No self-respecting dog would answer to a name like Arnold. It makes you sound wimpy."

The dog licked his hand.

"Unless your last name is Schwarzenegger."

Arnold whined.

Hell, Reed didn't want to care about a dog. Or

some kid who was wet behind the ears. Certainly not about a woman with the softest, sweetest lips he'd ever tasted.

She had no damn right sticking her nose into his business. He had enough on his plate worrying about Bets and the ranch.

"Señor Reed?"

He glanced toward the house. "What is it, Lupe?"

Heavy-footed, the housekeeper lumbered across the yard toward him, Bets propped comfortably against her full bosom. "My son, he called from Aledo."

"Texas? What's up?" With the back of his fingers, he stroked Bets's silky cap of hair.

"His wife, she is sick. I've got to go back and take care of their kids so he can keep working."

He frowned. "How long you planning to be gone?" He'd be able to manage for a few days, maybe a week.

"I'm no coming back, *señor*."

That news staggered him. "Wait a minute. You can't just up and go. Who'll take care of Bets while *I'm* working?"

"It's family." She shrugged as if that explained everything. "I'll take the morning bus to Los Angeles. You'll find somebody else for Betina."

Sure he would, Reed thought. But how long was it going to take? And how the hell was he going to finish putting in that fence and handle all his other chores when he didn't have anybody to look after Bets?

ANN HAD NEVER BEEN so relieved to get home to her sanctuary, to some renewed sense of security. Once inside, she twisted the dead bolt shut, drew a deep breath and rubbed the back of her hand across her mouth. His flavor was still there. Deep down, she suspected it always would be. Her moral aversion to infidelity didn't carry an ounce of weight with her overactive hormones.

Maybe he wasn't married, she thought in desperation. Surely Mr. Dunlap—or someone—would have mentioned...

But she was only rationalizing, and she knew it.

Dropping her briefcase and the box that she'd exchanged at Dora's onto the coffee table, Ann plopped down on the couch. She leaned back and stared up at the beamed ceiling.

So much for priding herself on her self-control. Obviously she hadn't learned a thing in the past thirteen years about keeping her runaway passions in check. At least not when a reckless cowboy was involved. One simple kiss and she'd very nearly forgotten every lesson she'd ever learned.

Well, perhaps the kiss hadn't been all that simple, she conceded. Expert was closer to the truth. Relentless.

She'd wanted so much to rip off his hat and thread her fingers through the thick silkiness of his hair. Had ached to feel his arms fully embrace her, drawing her body against the hard length of his. In secret, rebellious places she had flowed with the miracle of desire, a miracle she had denied herself for a long time.

And would continue to deny as long as she had an iota of good sense. That wasn't likely to be long if she was around Reed again anytime soon.

She'd have to find someone else to help Jason, that was all. Reed wasn't interested. She could hardly blame him. She'd overstepped her bounds by even asking.

And she'd paid the price.

At least this time the consequences hadn't been as costly as her adolescent folly when she'd run off with another unrepentant bad boy, Shane Edwards. It hadn't taken her long to realize she'd made a terrible mistake. All he'd wanted to do was drink and carouse, and when she objected, he'd simply moved out of their dingy motel room, deserting her. By then it was too late.

She was pregnant.

Dear God, what a fool she'd been.

Her throat tightened and tears sprang to her eyes. Instinctively she placed her palm on her stomach. After all these years she still remembered the most painful lesson of all.

She'd lost the baby, miscarrying within days of her return home.

On the rare occasions when she allowed herself to think about the baby, the hollow, burning ache was still there. The emptiness. The terrible sense of loss and grief. She doubted anyone who hadn't experienced a miscarriage could understand her lingering sorrow.

Her chin quivered, and she pursed her lips to halt the flow of emotion.

Certainly her parents had only felt relief. Their daughter's pristine reputation could be restored.

With a determined sigh, she leaned forward and picked up Dora's Dream Man box. Maybe if she could get the miniature medieval knight in its proper place on her mantel, her whole life would settle back to where it belonged—back to a calm, conservative routine.

An occasionally lonely routine, she admitted with characteristic honesty.

She lifted the lid and stared at the lead figure nestled carefully in the foam padding. Her heart contracted.

"No, this can't be happening to me. It can't. It's a terrible mistake."

The cowboy was still there—chambray shirt, chaps, mounted on a sorrel cow pony, his stained Stetson right beside him. But this time he was carrying a baby up against his shoulder. To compound the image, in one corner of the box there was a raggedy-looking black-and-white dog, its tail poised to signal the animal's pleasure at trotting along beside his master when he whistled.

There was no woman in the picture. None.

Somehow in the confusion at Dora's store when she'd been helping the customer find the Custer display, Ann had picked up the wrong box. She hadn't checked again. Now it was too late.

For a long time, she didn't move. She barely breathed. She simply stared at the Dream Man she didn't dare to want.

Chapter Four

Cradling Bets in one arm, Reed managed to dial the phone. He'd driven Lupe into town early that morning, where she'd gotten on a bus for L.A. Now he needed to find a replacement for her so he could get on with his own work.

Not that he wouldn't mind being a full-time daddy to Bets, he thought, brushing a kiss on her cheek. But somebody had to earn a living around here. Looked like he was elected.

On the third ring, a woman answered. "Del Oro employment agency."

"Yeah, I'm looking to hire a housekeeper, a live-in if you've got one."

"Those positions are difficult to fill, sir, but I'd certainly be happy to take your request." She sounded nice, very professional.

"Okay, but I need one in a hurry. I've got a kid, see? She's only a month old and I need someone to take care of her while I'm working."

"I quite understand. Finding proper child care is a difficult problem." She paused, and he heard papers being shuffled around. "Now then, your name, sir?"

"Reed Drummond. I own the Rocking D Ranch a couple of miles inland from town. I don't care about age or race or anything like that. Just somebody who'll be good with the baby."

The pause was longer this time. "You're Max Drummond's son?" she asked, her voice hesitant, almost accusing.

"Yeah, but what's that got to do with—"

"Mr. Drummond, both you and your father have a reputation—"

"My ol' man's dead."

"—such that, in good conscience, I would be reluctant to refer any decent woman—"

"What the hell are you saying? That I'm not good enough to hire a damn housekeeper?"

"Really, Mr. Drummond, there's no need to shout."

In a delayed reaction to his raised voice, Bets's eyes flew open, and she began to cry.

He adjusted the baby's position, lifting her to his shoulder, trying to pat her back with one hand while not dropping the phone. He lowered his voice. "Now look, lady, you can't discriminate. My money is as good as—"

"Good day, Mr. Drummond." The phone went dead.

"Ah, hell!" He slammed down the phone.

Bets' frightened wail increased in volume.

"Ah, come on, sweet pea," he crooned. "Daddy didn't mean to scare you." He jiggled her up and down, pacing across the kitchen to the window that looked out toward the distant ocean. The movement seemed to calm her, her cry turning to little sucking sounds as her head relaxed against the crook of his neck.

She was definitely the softest, sweetest thing he'd ever known. But what the devil was he going to do with her if he couldn't find a housekeeper?

Mar del Oro only had one employment agency, and that one was a bust.

When he called the agencies in San Luis Obispo, they weren't much more help, saying they didn't normally refer clients that far away. Without giving him any encouragement, they took his request. Reed suspected they tossed the form in the trash as soon as they hung up.

His next choice was to place an ad in the local weekly newspaper, but that wouldn't appear for several days.

When Bets woke from her morning nap, he bent over to change her diaper and said, "Looks like you're stuck with me, sweet pea. Where I go, you go."

Her big, brown eyes focusing on Reed, she pumped her tiny legs and waved her arms.

He grinned. "Good. I'm glad you don't mind 'cause I've got lots of work to do." Including finishing the fencing job down at the school.

His smile hitched up another notch. Maybe sweet sugar-Annie would be interested in the job he had to offer, particularly if he included a few nonstandard benefits in the employment package, ones they could both enjoy.

ANN NOTICED HIM during the morning snack break.

Naturally, she ignored him.

Naturally, the girls in her class didn't.

"He's got his *baby* with him this morning, Ms. Forrester," Rosetta said, all agog. "She's *sooo* sweet."

"He's carrying her in one of those sling things," Hailey Hunter chimed in. "Right up against his chest like my mom did with my baby brother."

"While he's digging holes for the fence?" Ann asked, stunned as she pictured a tiny baby huddled against the broad expanse of his chest.

The girls nodded enthusiastically.

Why on earth would he bring a baby with him, exposing the poor thing to all that dust and dirt out in the field? Not to mention cuddling an infant against his sweaty, muscular body—which she shouldn't be thinking about.

It was none of her concern, she told herself as she brought the class to order. Reed was the child's father. Within reason, he had a right to do whatever he wanted with the baby. Surely he wouldn't harm the child in any way. And a little dust and dirt probably wouldn't hurt. Babies were resilient, she'd been told.

She was still telling herself that when lunch period started, and she found herself walking out past the football field to where Reed was working.

Arnold spotted her right away. He came loping

toward her, his tail flagging. As she petted him, he licked her hand, and a lump formed in her throat. She'd left the miniature on her kitchen table, the cowboy with his baby and his dog. She'd eaten breakfast staring at the darn thing, almost afraid to touch it for fear the entire tableau would suddenly come alive in full-size and living color.

And now it had, though Reed wasn't mounted on Fiero. He'd brought the pickup again. But he was carrying the baby in a blue mother's sling, and the dog had been right beside him.

Nervously, her mouth dry, she brushed her hair back behind her shoulder. "Do you think it's a good idea for the baby to be out here in all this heat and dust?"

Arnold trotted back to his master and flopped down in a circle of trampled grass, the fragile spring wildflowers bent flat.

Reed rested his arm on the posthole digger, giving Ann a lazy perusal with his burnished-bronze gaze before he spoke. "She got fussy in the car seat."

Her gaze slid to the truck and its open door. An infant carrier was carefully strapped into the passenger seat. "Couldn't your wife have—"

"I don't have a wife."

An unwelcome flutter of combined relief and excitement rippled through her stomach. "The woman I saw last night—"

"My housekeeper. She quit. Took the first bus out of town this morning."

"The baby's mother—"

"Dead. So's her father. I'm adopting her."

Ann's jaw went slack. She never would have thought—

"I trust you don't have any objections to me adopting this baby, sugar, 'cause it wouldn't do you any good. She's mine." He staked his claim as firmly as a rancher would mark the boundaries of his land, making sure trespassers knew they weren't welcome.

"Object? No, I'm just surprised. I mean, I assumed—"

"That I'm not good enough?"

She bristled. "Of course not." But she was amazed he'd want to saddle himself with an infant. That hardly fit the image she had of Reed Drummond, a restless, reckless cowboy who didn't want any roots.

"The employment agency I called this morning sure wasn't interested in finding somebody to replace Lupe. Seems they didn't think much of my reputation. Or my old man's." The baby made a soft, crying sound. Attentive to the baby's needs, he shifted her slightly, turning his body so he shaded her from the direct sun.

Ann marveled at his gentleness, the way his large hands cradled the child, and an ache tightened in her chest. "I'm sure you'll be able to find someone soon."

"Think so?" He tipped his hat to reveal more of his face, and he gave her a wicked grin. "I don't suppose you'd consider taking the job. To sweeten the deal, I could offer some extra fringe *benefits*."

Ann had no doubts about what those *benefits*

would include. She wanted no part of them. "Thank you, but I like the job I have."

"Well, ain't that a darn shame," he drawled.

Heat flooded her cheeks but she wouldn't give him the satisfaction of letting him know just how strongly he affected her. "Have you given any more thought to mentoring Jason?"

"As you can see, my plate's plenty full right now, sugar-Annie. Bets, here, is my first priority." He indicated the baby huddled close to his chest.

"Yes, I can understand that." She could even respect his decision. Certainly she admired his willingness to adopt a child, particularly an infant. Not many single men would do that. She had to wonder why Reed had, and what his connection was to the baby.

But none of that solved her problem with Jason. He hadn't come to school today. One of his foster brothers had said he'd gotten as far as the school's front gate that morning, and then he'd taken off to parts unknown.

She hoped he hadn't made good on his threat to head for Los Angeles. Assuming he managed to arrive there safely, Ann very much doubted that his mother would welcome him.

The school bell sounded twice, a call for the janitor, and Ann realized lunch period was nearly over. If she was going to survive a full afternoon schedule of classes, she'd have to eat something in a hurry.

"I have to go," she said, taking a few backward steps away from Reed, oddly reluctant to leave him.

"Well, now, y'all come back and visit any time,

sweet sugar." His cocky grin creased his cheek. "Bets and me are always happy to have a pretty little lady like you drop by, you hear?"

She turned and fled before he could see the heat racing up her neck to color her cheeks. But that didn't stop her blush. All the way back to the main building, she could feel his hot gaze on her. Intimately. Warming far more than her face.

ANN MET HER PARENTS that evening at the Blue Moon Saloon, the nicest restaurant in town, which specialized in fresh fish and French cuisine. They were waiting out front with the new bank manager, David Emery Curtis III, and they chatted while waiting for the next available table.

"I understand you're a teacher," David said. "That's very admirable."

"Most days it's simply hard work," she replied, smiling. He was definitely a David—not a Dave or Davie or, heaven forbid, a Butch or Stinky. In his late thirties, he was perfectly groomed in a dark suit and power tie, his blond hair precisely combed, his back ramrod straight. Small, round glasses adorned a face with features so even he might have modeled for the "after" photo in a plastic surgeon's gallery of fabulous successes. All and all, David Emery Curtis III was the epitome of a man you could trust to guard your money with care.

A rebellious part of Ann's mind considered that Reed Drummond was exactly the opposite, and therefore all the more intriguing to a woman who should know better.

"Banking has its moments, too," he commented.

Her mother said, "You know, David is new in town and hasn't had time to make many friends yet."

"He has a great future in the banking business," Ann's father commented. "He comes from a long line of successful financiers."

"I believe your parents are attempting a little matchmaking, Miss Forrester." His wry smile was a gentle one, nothing like the raffish grin that had been troubling her dreams of late. "Should we be insulted or indulge them?"

She laughed. At least he had a sense of humor. "Oh, let's indulge them, why don't we? They won't be able to stand the shock."

Her parents vociferously sputtered their denials, but they'd already been found out. Relaxing, she glanced around the well-lit parking lot, which was adjacent to the only supermarket in town. The evening air was warm, tinged with a hint of salt from the nearby ocean, and the press of tourist cars on the street had slowed to a trickle.

Her breath caught. As if her thoughts of Reed had conjured him up out of thin air, she saw him lifting his baby out of the infant carrier in his truck and fastening her securely in the sling across his chest. He looked up then and their eyes met.

The moment was electric, the sparks leaping between them like a physics experiment gone awry. The contrast between his rugged masculinity and the gentle way he cared for his baby daughter left her transfixed. Lust and wonder mixed in a volatile combination in her chest, threatening to explode. What woman wouldn't be tempted by such a complex man?

He tipped his Stetson to her. "Evenin', sugarAnnie," he drawled, slow and silky smooth, sexy as you please. "Nice night, isn't it?"

Stunned by her powerful reaction to the man, she could barely nod in response. Other parts of her anatomy had a far more dramatic rejoinder, however—like hot, molten liquid flowing through her veins.

"You don't know that man, do you, Ann Marie?" her father hissed as Reed turned and strolled toward the grocery store, his long legs leisurely covering the distance in easy strides.

"I, ah...he's been doing some work around the school." Her mouth was as dry as the parched hills in summer, her stomach as knotted as a Chinese puzzle. "Building a fence."

"Well, you keep your distance from him, missy. That's Reed Drummond, back from wherever he ran off to years ago. He's nothing but trouble, you hear?"

Ann didn't need to be told Reed meant trouble for a woman. Intellectually, she knew that. But some part of her that was totally unrelated to her brain reacted to Reed as she had never reacted to any other man, not even the bad boy she'd fallen for as an adolescent.

Her parents had both been devastated by her brief rebellion, her father even more than her mother. His "baby angel" had shown she had feet of clay. Ever since then he had been wary of any man she met—though they were few and far between.

She could hardly imagine what his reaction might be if he knew Reed had actually kissed her. And not only had she enjoyed it, in her most secret self she wanted him to do it again.

With a sigh, she looked up at David Emery Curtis III. However pleasant he might be, she knew he'd never be able to set off the sparks in her the way Reed could with a single raffish grin.

More's the pity, she thought grimly.

IN THE GROCERY STORE, Reed juggled Bets in one arm as he loaded his cart with diapers, milk, beer and makings for sandwiches. He figured sweet sugar-Annie was probably planning something a little more gourmet for her evening meal than what he had in mind. That was okay. Blowing money on fancy food didn't fill him up any more than the basics did.

"Drummond? Is that you?"

Reed turned to see who had called him. "John? John Fuentes? Hey, man, how's it going?"

"Can't complain." John shook his hand. He had a slightly crooked smile and a nose to match, one that had been broken in a failed effort to score the winning touchdown for Del Oro High in a league play-off game. His dark eyes flashed with the same spark of assurance Reed had noted when he'd been a kid admiring John, the upper classman and school hero. When John had been in the principal's office receiving accolades, Reed had been there serving detention. "I heard you'd moved back to the ranch.

"Yep. The proverbial bad penny."

John checked the baby in his arm. "A penny and change, it looks to me."

"Something like that." He adjusted Bets's position to his shoulder. "I figured you'd be long gone from this backwater town by now." Reed had heard John had gotten a college scholarship, for academics, not athletics. In fact, in high school he'd been a little undersized for a jock. He'd filled out now and looked rock hard.

"I spent some time in L.A.," John admitted, pulling his grocery cart out of the way so a customer could pass in the narrow aisle. "But I had a chance to come home and jumped at it."

"That's great. Maybe we'll be able to do some business together." John looked so prosperous in his sports coat and tie that Reed suspected he might own a small business in town.

John laughed, an infectious sound that had the ladies turning their heads. "You'd better hope not, Drummond. I'm the town's new police chief."

"You're kidding."

"'Fraid not. I spent eight years on the force in L.A., worked my way up to lieutenant and then the job opened up here around the first of the year. I couldn't pass it up. If I had, Mama would have tanned my hide." His eyes sparkled with amusement that his mother would have so much influence over her thirty-year-old son...a cop at that.

"I'll be damned." Smiling, Reed shook his head.

If there had been railroad tracks through Mar del Oro, John would have been raised on the wrong side of them. And look what he'd accomplished. It made Reed feel guilty he'd wasted so many years himself. But he was back now, too, and he had Bets.

John extended his hand again. "Good to see you, Drummond. Maybe one of these days I'll drop by the Rocking D—just to say hello."

"Sure. Anytime." He didn't know if John was saying that because he remembered Reed had been less than a model citizen as a kid and was afraid he'd start a crime wave in town or if the new police chief was really offering his hand in friendship. It didn't matter. Reed's nose was as clean as they got. He wasn't about to get so much as a speeding ticket, not while he had Bets to worry about. And anything more than a ticket would play hob with his petition to adopt Bets.

REED DIDN'T GET much sleep during the next few nights; he didn't get much work done during the day, either.

Only one woman had answered his ad in the local paper. A witch.

She glanced around the living room, her nose in the air like she was the damn queen of Transylvania, for God's sake. "This is simply not up to my standards," she announced, sneering. With that, she turned and stalked out of the house.

Good riddance, Reed decided. He wouldn't have wanted that old biddy to come within a mile of Bets anyway. The poor kid would probably get hives.

And so what if the house wasn't furnished with the fanciest stuff around, the stove was old, there was no dishwasher and a few springs were broken in the couch. He'd gotten the place cleaned up; he'd scrubbed the floors and washed the walls until his hands had turned to prunes. He might not have a lot of money but his daughter wasn't going to grow up in filth like he had after his mom had run off. Reed had been ten at the time.

The memory of her abandonment still had the power to knock the air right out of his lungs.

When nobody else responded to the ad, he asked some of the junior high girls if they had an older sister who might want to baby-sit after school. Even a few hours a day would have helped.

You would have thought Reed was a serial rapist the way their mothers reacted. One woman had actually accused him on the phone of trying to lure her sweet innocent daughter to his house in order to seduce her. She'd sent the police chief around to give him a hard time.

Damn! Reed wasn't into robbing cradles. He had a baby to take care of. What the hell did they expect him to do? Fortunately, Fuentes had realized the woman had gone off half-cocked.

In frustration, he speared his fingers through his hair. Maybe he could advertise in an L.A. paper. He wasn't averse to hiring a new immigrant, legal or not, and he'd even consider hiring a married couple. He sure as hell could use an extra hand around here.

The phone rang. He picked it up on the first ring for fear the sound would wake Bets. "Yeah?"

"Mr. Drummond? This is Dr. Richmond from Fort Worth General Hospital."

Reed remembered the doctor's voice, the one who had been there when Betsy died. Fear knotted in his gut. Had they found out something was wrong with Bets? A problem that hadn't shown up when she was in the hospital?

"Is there a problem with the baby?" he asked abruptly, turning to find a piece of paper on the kitchen counter to write on in case he needed to make notes.

"Not exactly, at least nothing medical. How is she doing?"

"Seems fine to me."

"Have you taken her in for a checkup yet?"

"I've got an appointment scheduled," he lied. He knew from the books he'd borrowed from the library that she needed a six-week exam. He fully intended to see that happened. He just hadn't made the call yet.

"Well, she seemed quite robust and healthy at the time of birth. I'm sure she's fine. But I'm calling for another reason."

His forehead tightened with a frown. Doctors didn't call up former patients—or their parents—to pass the time of day. "What's that?"

"A woman from the state adoption agency dropped by to see me this morning. It seems there's some question about whether you are a suitable adoptive parent for Betina."

The pencil he was holding nearly snapped, he was gripping it so tightly. "Her mother wanted me to raise her. Isn't that a good enough reason for me to adopt her?"

"At the time, I found it quite acceptable, and I'm confident you'll be a fine parent for her. Otherwise, I would not have recommended releasing her into your custody."

"Now you're having second thoughts?"

"Not at all. I simply wanted to warn you that the adoptions people will be asking the social services office in your county to do a background investigation on you and the home situation you're providing for Betina."

"She's got a good home." Better than he'd ever had. Reed would make sure of that.

"I think they may be concerned about, well, what sort of a mother figure she'll have in her life. My intent is not to be insulting, Mr. Drummond, but I got the impression this morning that the authorities may have some doubts about your character and stability. I gather you were a hired hand for some years with no permanent address."

"I'm as stable as they come." Now that he'd settled down, it would take dynamite to blow him off the Rocking D.

"Again, I don't mean to pry, but is someone else helping to care for Betina? A woman, perhaps?"

"I had a housekeeper," he said gruffly. "She quit on me but I'm looking for a new one." And the search was going damn slow. What the hell would the bureaucrats think of an illegal immigrant, he wondered. Probably not much.

"Yes, well, I think they'd look more favorably on you if you were married—"

"Married!" He nearly choked on the word.

"—to a woman with an impeccable reputation. The authorities would hardly find room to quibble with you about adopting Betina if that were the case."

He slammed the pencil down on the counter. "I'm a good father to Bets. How the hell can they ask for more than that?"

"I know it sounds unreasonable, and you may well be able to make a good case for yourself. But knowing how governments work, I thought I'd warn you."

"Yeah, well, thanks for calling. It really made my day."

"I'm sorry, Mr. Drummond. And good luck."

The authorities damn well could quibble all they liked, he thought as he hung up the phone. He was Bets's daddy. That's what Betsy had wanted and that's how it was gonna be.

THE FOLLOWING DAY a letter came in the mail from the San Luis Obispo County, Department of Adoptions. It informed Reed his petition to adopt Betina Shoemaker was under review, and he could expect a social worker to visit within the next seven to ten working days for a home study. He would be asked to provide three local character references who would testify that he was a suitable parent.

Damn! There weren't three people in the whole country, much less in Mar del Oro, who'd make a statement like that. It'd be just the opposite, in fact. Most of the people in town would be happy to tell a nosy social worker that he was the last man on earth who'd make a decent father.

Furious, he wadded up the letter and fired it across the living room. Tears ached in his throat and burned in his eyes.

Betina was the best thing that had ever happened in his life. He'd do anything to keep her.

Including marriage, if it came to that.

Standing, he walked into Bets's room and stared down at her asleep in the crib he'd bought from a used furniture store. He'd made a mobile out of a clothes hanger and some old baseball cards to hang above the crib, and tacked a poster of Snoopy on the wall. Not much of a nursery, he supposed, but Bets didn't seem to care. He'd buy her nice stuff later, when the ranch was back on its feet and making money again. Anything Bets wanted.

The only woman he knew with an impeccable reputation was sweet sugar-Annie. He wouldn't mind having her in his bed, he admitted, but he doubted she'd be thrilled at the prospect of marrying him. From what he'd seen of her at the restaurant the other night, she went for guys in suits. Reed didn't even own one.

He rubbed the back of his fingers across Bets's downy-smooth cheek.

The only way Ann Forrester would marry him was if it was a temporary arrangement and he had something to trade, something she thought was damn important.

SQUATTING BESIDE the flower bed, Ann used a trowel to scoop out a hole for the clump of pansies she'd bought at the nursery. She was late with her spring planting this year, and the yard looked colorless without fresh bedding plants to line the walkway to the porch.

She'd vowed this would be the weekend she'd get it done, and trays of snapdragons, marigolds and pansies rested on the brick path waiting to be planted.

Her home was in the hills above the town of Mar del Oro, where the houses were modest, the yards well kept, and the neighbors friendly. Mothers felt comfortable having their children play outside since everyone kept an eye on them.

As she was tamping the loose dirt around the plant, she heard a truck driving up the street. It stopped at the curb behind her, and a prickle of unease edged down her spine. The only person she knew with a pickup was Reed Drummond.

Still squatting, she swiveled in time to see him circling the truck to the passenger side. Her heart rate accelerated, and she tried to remain calm, shading her eyes against the glare of the sun with her hand. Why was he here? What did he want? More to the point, what did *she* want?

She'd finally moved the cowboy miniature to the fireplace mantel. She'd told herself she was too embarrassed to take the piece back to Dora a second time, and it was a beautifully artistic creation, one worthy of display. But she suspected she had an ulterior motive she didn't care to examine too closely.

With ease of experience, he lifted the baby to his shoulder and hooked a diaper bag on his arm. With one slim, cowboy hip, he slammed the door shut. His expression was grim.

Standing, she tugged off her gardening gloves and tucked them into the hip pocket of her jeans. Her baggy T-shirt was streaked with dirt, the knees of her pants muddy. Not wanting to fuss with her appearance that morning, she'd pulled her hair back into a ponytail and applied only a smidgen of makeup, enough to get her by for the quick trip to the nursery.

Reed gave her his patented once-over, the one that made her skin flush and her breath crowd in her chest. "Very nice, teach," he drawled. "I didn't think you were the kind who enjoyed getting down and dirty." His brows rose just enough so she knew exactly what he meant by "down and dirty."

She ignored the implication. "I enjoy *gardening*."

His lips slipped into a wry smile. She hadn't fooled him. He was reading her like a book—very likely an erotic one, fully illustrated. In color.

"Was there something you wanted?" she snapped waspishly.

"Oh, yeah." He slid his gaze away from her to glance up and down the street. Two youngsters were in-line skating across the way, and Ann's neighbor was washing his car in the driveway. Farther on, a couple of adolescents were shooting hoops at a basket attached above the garage door. "This is a little public for what I have in mind. How 'bout we go inside?''

Her heart rate stumbled. Just what did he have in mind? And did she want to know?

"You asked a favor of me, teach. Now I've got one to ask of you." He adjusted his hold on the baby and headed up the walkway.

Ann had little choice but to follow. In spite of his outrageous remarks and flirtatious manner, it appeared Reed was here about mentoring Jason. She could hardly send him away when the boy needed so much help. Reed's visit wasn't anything personal.

But being alone with him in her living room felt very much personal.

He filled the space, not just because of his size but because of his swaggering presence even when he was standing still. Ann wondered how he could give that impression, particularly with a baby tucked against his shoulder. Somehow his rugged masculinity overwhelmed everything around him.

Willing herself to break the heavy silence in the room, she asked, "How did you know where I live?"

"A. Forrester. You're in the phone book."

She'd always thought it important to be available to her students if they needed her. In the future, though, she'd consider an unlisted number. "I assume you're here because you've decided to mentor Jason."

"I'll do it."

Tension eased from her shoulders. "That's wonderful. I'm sure Jason will—"

"But I need something from you in return."

She eyed him uneasily, noting the way his big hand rested protectively on the baby's back, soothing the infant. Oddly, she thought if Reed chose to be, he'd be a very gentle lover, not rough or harsh as his appearance might suggest. Almost tender.

She licked her lips, recalling the taste of his kiss—potent but not at all gentle. "What is it you want from me, Reed?"

"It's not what I *want*, sugar-Annie. It's what I *need*."

Her eyes widened.

"I need you to marry me."

Chapter Five

Never in her wildest imaginings had Ann expected to hear those words from Reed Drummond.

"Marriage isn't a laughing matter," she said. Her knees had gone weak at his proposal—if that's what it could be called—but she wasn't about to collapse in a dither over what was more likely an obscene suggestion.

"You're right. The whole institution stinks. But I need a wife."

"What on earth for? If you're talking about sex—"

"I figure we can negotiate the conjugal rights part, but I guarantee it wouldn't be a hardship on you."

"How romantic," she countered. "I can't recall the last time I had such a tender proposal."

"So that's why you haven't accepted any of them?"

His remark was like a slap across her face. She'd *never* had a proposal. The rebellious bad boy she'd run off with thirteen years ago hadn't considered marriage. Even if he'd known she was pregnant, he wouldn't have stuck around. Since then, she'd avoided intimate relationships. She hadn't been able to trust her own judgement. She couldn't now.

"That's none of your damn business."

He ignored her as he juggled the baby and diaper bag, retrieving a flannel blanket, which he spread across one of the cushions on her couch. He laid the baby down on her back.

In spite of herself, Ann was fascinated by how carefully he cared for his child, for all the world as if he were the infant's biological father. "Are you sure she won't roll off?" she asked, her experience with babies limited to those her friends had borne.

"They can't roll from their backs to their fronts till they're at least a couple of months old, usually later. But I still watch her real good."

The baby stretched and cooed contentedly, her gaze searching through the unfamiliar environment for something colorful to focus on. This was Ann's first close-up of the baby. She had a cap of dark hair, not unlike Reed's, and her cheeks were chubby despite her delicate size. The pale pink stretch outfit she wore was too big, the excess fabric flapping freely beyond the limits of her limbs like a clown's shoes.

She was adorable, and Ann suddenly ached to pick her up and cuddle her. It had been a long time since she'd dreamed—

"Like I told you, I'm trying to adopt Bets, but the damn bureaucrats are planning to give me a hard time. My reputation isn't exactly the best around here." He gave a self-deprecating shrug which held not an ounce of remorse. "If I can't come up with a wife, one who's got a reputation that's a hell of lot better than mine, they're going to take Bets away from me. That's not going to happen."

"Are you asking me to *arrange* a marriage for you to some—"

"You're it, sweet sugar. I don't have time to mess around *arranging* anything."

"Well, you're sadly mistaken if you think I'd consider marrying you."

"I'm not talking about a lifetime commitment. I only need a wife until the bureaucrats approve Bets's adoption. Then you'd be free to go on your merry way."

"That's insulting."

"In return, I'll do what I can to straighten out Jason for you."

But at what price? The shock wasn't so much that Reed would make such a proposition, but that she would consider it even for one single millisecond. Which she wasn't going to do.

She walked to the door and opened it. "I think you'd better go."

He didn't budge but continued to stand by the couch, his stance wide-legged and aggressive. "Betina's mother was Betsy Shoemaker. She was eighteen and so was her boyfriend. They'd both run away from a group foster home, mostly because she was being hassled by one of her would-be keepers. The two of them bummed around the country, picking up what work they could. In their whole lives, they never had anything. Not decent parents and sure as hell not much money. But they had each other, and then they were going to have a baby.

"I don't know why, but they latched on to me like I was a surrogate big brother, or something. I didn't ask for it. But they stuck to me like glue, followed me from job to job. I couldn't get rid of them.

"They had this old jalopy they drove around in. The brakes were half busted and the tires bald. I told 'em they ought to dump the damn thing but they wouldn't listen. They were saving money so Betsy could have her baby in the hospital." He glanced down at the infant, and though his eyes softened, his jaw was tight.

"One day they were driving along a country road and ran into one of those gully-washer rains that come down so hard you can't see ten feet in front of your face. They plowed into a parked big rig that hadn't gotten all the way off the road.

"Tommy died at the scene. I got Betsy out of the car but she was all broken up. At the hospital, they had to choose between her and the baby. Betsy made the decision. It was the most courageous—"

His voice broke. He looked away, swiping at his face with his arm.

Ann had been listening motionless, mesmerized by his story. She almost went to him then, to console him in his grief. Dear heaven! He'd witnessed the accident and tried to rescue his friends.

But she wasn't sure of the reception she'd get. Reed wasn't a man who was used to showing his emotions. She suspected he'd be embarrassed if she made any special note of them. And her own feelings were so on edge, she was near tears herself. Her heart ached for Betsy and Tommy, Reed, too, and little Betina.

"Betsy wanted me to raise her baby," he said, his voice low and taut when he'd brought himself back under control. His eyes glistened. "That's what I intend to do—one way or another."

Ann didn't doubt his resolve for a moment. If need be, he'd run off with the baby and raise her on the road as his own. "But marriage. That's such a drastic step. Isn't there any other way?"

"Dammit, don't you think I've racked my brain trying to come up with something else that makes sense?" Almost desperately, he scooped up the infant and crossed the room to Ann. The front door was still open and a slight breeze ruffled the baby's hair. "Look at her, sugar. Hold her and then tell me you wouldn't do anything in the world to keep her if you were in my shoes."

"My hands are dirty. I can't—"

"Bets won't mind."

He thrust the baby into Ann's arms.

Her emotions were like quicksilver as the infant snuggled close and rooted against her breast. It was as if Reed had given her back the child she had lost. Her heart ached, and she had difficulty drawing a breath. Stroking Betina's soft cap of hair, Ann looked at her through a veil from the past.

How many years, how much grief had she'd tried to bury amid her own broken dreams?

Was it possible that this time she could have it all, the hot sultry passion she'd felt so explosively when she was with Reed? And motherhood, too? Could she accept his proposition without his love? And then only temporarily. How would she ever be able to walk away without losing her heart both to the man and to this precious little baby?

Lifting her head, she looked at him, trying to puzzle out the answer as though it were hidden in the sharp angles and planes of Reed's face, in the intensity of his burnished eyes. The answer came to her more easily than she expected.

She had to give herself the chance, give Reed and Betina the chance. The notion was both simple and wildly risky. And in the bargain Jason would gain a mentor—though Ann admitted that minor victory was only a small part of her motivation.

"How soon do you need to get married?" she asked.

The tension around his sensual lips eased ever so slightly. "Next week. The sooner the better."

Her mind reeled. "That isn't much time to plan—"

"We can get the license on Monday and get married on Wednesday. If the adoption people show up before that, I'll figure a way to hold them off."

"You could tell them we're...engaged." She nearly choked on the word. It didn't come close to describing their unorthodox relationship. From Reed's perspective, he'd probably say theirs was a business agreement to skirt unfair adoption regulations. She was less sure how to describe her own feelings.

"Knowing the government, they'll show up in their own sweet time trying to make me sweat." He ran his hand along the back of his neck where his saddle-brown hair swept the top of his blue collar. "Have you got a minister or judge you can ask to do the deed?"

"Yes, I, uh, guess so." Unless she came to her senses by then. But she'd already cast her lot with Reed. For her, there'd be no turning back.

"Okay, that's settled then."

"I take it you're not planning an extended honeymoon?"

His lips twitched with the threat of a smile, and he eyed her with blatant male appreciation. "You ready to negotiate the conjugal rights part now?"

A lump of anticipation thickened in her throat. "I'd being lying if I didn't admit there was a certain...sexual chemistry between us."

His smile broadened. "I *do* like an honest woman."

"Besides," she hastened to add, her mind rationalizing her impulsive decision, "if you draw a perceptive social worker, she's bound to recognize this hasty marriage you've conjured up is phony if we haven't, uh, been intimate. She might deny your petition to adopt Bets." *Oh, Lord! What had she just said? Agreed to?*

"It's a real nice thing you're doing, sweet sugar-Annie. And I promise, you can look forward to our wedding night."

Her legs did go weak then, and she clung to Betina more tightly. This was madness. Any moment now an army of psychiatrists was going to show up and take her away in a straitjacket. Somewhere out there a padded cell had her name on it.

"What time do you get off work Monday?" he asked.

"School's out at two-thirty, but I usually—"

"I'll pick you up then. We'll have to drive to San Luis Obispo, and I want to get there in plenty of time before the office closes."

"Bossy, aren't you? What about blood tests?"

His brows tugged together. "I gave blood for Betsy. I'll have the doc there fax me the results. How 'bout you?"

Ann thought a moment, almost too on edge to concentrate. "I had a strep infection during the spring break. The students are particularly adept at sharing their germs with their teachers. Dr. Avery drew some blood. I'm sure he'll give me the report."

Reed seemed to think that would be satisfactory. "Could I have Bets back now?" He held out his hands, rough and calloused, gifted with incredible gentleness for his daughter.

She wanted to tell Reed no. She wanted to hold the baby a little longer, to feel her soft skin and confirm she had the appropriate number of fingers and toes, just as a mother would do with her own newborn. *A mother who had never seen her own child.*

"Of course." Clearing the clog of emotion from her throat, Ann handed Bets back to her daddy.

He gathered up the diaper bag, and with his daughter snuggled against his shoulder, Reed left.

Ann watched him walk to his truck. She'd just agreed to marry a virtual stranger, and he hadn't so much as said goodbye, much less expressed anything like gratitude. Or affection. And yet she wanted this man as fiercely as she'd wanted anything in her entire life. It didn't even matter that he had no intention of making their marital arrangement permanent.

Heaven help her! Had she fallen in love with him already? After years of keeping a tight rein on her emotions, had Reed been the one to finally set them free?

Granted, a lot of what she was feeling was lust. But her emotions went deeper than that. In her heart she knew his bad-boy bravado, his arrogance, was only skin-deep. She'd seen him with Bets and knew in her soul that Reed Drummond was capable of giving all of the love he'd been denied as a child.

More than anything, she wanted to be on the receiving end when he finally realized the power of that uniquely human emotion.

She could only hope this swift collision between her heart and her good sense would be enduring enough to hold them together after the adoption people gave their blessing to Reed as Betina's daddy. Otherwise, he'd have no further use for Ann.

She worried her heart might not be able to withstand the double blow of his rejection…and losing another baby she'd already grown to love.

REED COULDN'T GET AWAY from Ann's place fast enough.

She'd started talking about a damn honeymoon, and all he could think about was starting it right then and there. On the living-room couch. Or on the floor. Hell, he didn't care. No way could he have made it to the bedroom if she had made a move on him.

He wanted her. Beneath him. Wrapped around him. Every which way he could get her.

Lust, that's all it was, he told himself. He'd enjoy it, sure. He'd been without a woman for a long time. But what he was doing was for Bets, for the promise he'd made to her mother. He wasn't going to get hung up in the marriage trap. Hell, he didn't have an ounce of mushy sentiment in him. Any softer side he might have had, had been beaten the hell out of him years ago, if not by his ol' man with a stick, then by his mother's desertion. Caring about another person was not a path he wanted to travel any time soon. Other than Bets. She was a different matter.

He whipped the truck onto the county road that led to his ranch.

Temporary. He'd made the arrangement clear to sweet sugar-Annie. She'd agreed. That was just fine with him. No one in his entire life had wanted more than that from him.

He slanted Bets a glance. She'd managed to find her finger and was tugging on it vigorously. In a minute, she'd set up a wail about being hungry.

He'd handle that as soon as he got home. It wouldn't be long.

He wondered how long his marriage to sugar-Annie would last. However long, he hoped he'd have his fill of her by the time she left. And hoped to God she wouldn't change her mind about the conjugal stuff.

"I WON'T HAVE IT, do you hear me?"

Ann had waited until Sunday to break the news of her forthcoming marriage to her parents. The delay hadn't forestalled her father's bellowing disapproval. She'd known it wouldn't.

"You don't have a choice, Daddy. I'm getting married Wednesday afternoon, and I'd like both you and Mother to be there."

"Of course we will, dear," her mother said, "but this all seems so—"

"No way in hell am I going to see you married to that...that man!" Her father didn't even bother to lower his voice, in spite of the fact all the windows were open and the neighbors were probably getting an earful. "I'd sooner see you an old maid."

"How thoughtful of you," she murmured. "Particularly, since by most standards I already *am* an old maid."

"Nonsense," he sputtered gruffly. "You just haven't found the right man yet. And that Drummond boy certainly isn't—"

"I think he is."

Her father's face turned bright red. If he'd had a heart condition, Ann would have been concerned, but she thought his reaction was mostly bluster and his own peculiar way of showing he loved her. When they'd bought this new house ten years ago, they'd even gone so far as to have a "guest cottage" built in the back. Ann was sure her parents had hoped she would live there after college rather than moving to her own place. She'd opted instead to use her modest inheritance from her maternal grandmother as a down payment on a house of her own.

"It all seems like such a rush, dear," her mother said. "Couldn't you wait a while? I'd always dreamed of you having a church wedding."

"I'm sorry, Mother." That dream had once been Ann's, too, but it didn't look like that was in the cards. "Judge Aldridge has agreed to perform the ceremony in his chambers at five on Wednesday. Since he's a friend of Father's—"

"He won't be a friend of mine one more day if he marries you to that no good—"

"Dad! Reed Drummond is going to be my husband whether or not you show up for the wedding." With as much dignity as she could muster, she rose to her feet. The living room of her parents' home had a cathedral ceiling and picture windows with an ocean view. The elegant ambiance had never felt so imposing, or more intimidating. Ann refused to be cowed. "And I intend to be the best wife I can be." Assuming Reed would give her the chance.

"You mark my words, Ann Marie," her father warned. "If you go through with this marriage to Reed Drummond, you'll regret it—just like you did the last time you ran off with a no-good scoundrel."

No words could have hurt her more. She'd made one mistake, and perhaps she was making another. But she desperately wanted her father's love and support, now more than ever. Instead, he'd thrown the past in her face.

Without wavering, she left the house. Her mother tried to stop her, but Ann shrugged her off. It was only when she reached her car and pulled the Mustang out of the driveway that she lost her composure. Within a half block, she had to pull to the curb as sobs burned in her chest and tears blurred her eyes.

She was about to marry a man whom not a single soul in Mar del Oro respected, or even trusted. Her heart told her it was the right thing to do, the only thing she could do.

Her head called her the worst kind of fool.

WHEN THE DISMISSAL bell sounded, Reed's truck was parked at the curb in front of the school. He slid out from behind the wheel when he saw Ann coming and held the driver's door open. He'd apparently finished the fencing job over the weekend and she hadn't seen him since his none-too-romantic proposal. As promised, however, he'd arrived at school promptly at two-thirty for their date to get the marriage license.

Their very first date, she thought with grim wryness, trembling on the inside. And they had an audience of about five hundred curious adolescents.

"Yo! Miz Forrester's got a boyfriend," Jason taunted. "Bet she's pretty hot stuff."

A gaggle of prepubescent girls coming out of the school gate giggled at the remark.

Ann ignored them.

Reed didn't. "Can it!" He sent the boy a fulminating look. To Ann, he said, "You'll have to get in from the driver's side. Bets's chair is strapped in over there."

She acknowledged his statement with a nod. But getting into the truck was no simple task. For reasons that now escaped her, she'd chosen to wear a suit with a straight skirt this morning. To step up into the cab, she'd have to hike her skirt so high, she'd be giving all and sundry a glimpse of her thighs—and then some, she suspected.

"Why don't we take my car?" she suggested, hoping to avoid making an immodest scene in front of half the student body.

Reed's eyes narrowed, his brows lowering as he took in her appearance from head to toe. "You would have been better off to wear your jeans," he muttered.

Before she could respond that since she'd never gotten a marriage license before she could hardly know the appropriate attire, he clasped her around the waist and lifted her as if she were no more bother than a sack of flour. She gasped and grabbed his forearms. They were rock hard, the muscles bunched in ribbons of steel.

For one brief moment, his thumbs skimmed the under side of her breasts, and then she was unceremoniously seated behind the wheel of the truck. But the heat stayed where his hands had been, a sensual brand that promised more to come.

Their gazes locked. Open lust narrowed the band of bronze in his eyes, and Ann's mouth went dry. At least he was feeling some of the same volatile reaction she was experiencing. She'd hate to think the physical attraction she'd so foolishly admitted to was one-sided.

"Scoot over," he ordered gruffly.

Moving wasn't easy, and Ann's paralysis wasn't due entirely to her tight skirt. It had more to do with the heavy tension that filled the air between them.

There was no relief when they got under way, either. Three abreast, Ann was mashed between the infant seat where Bets slept contentedly and Reed's big, lanky body. She tried to concentrate on the baby, adjusting the light flannel blanket that covered her, but she was riotously aware that she was thigh to thigh with Reed. His heat seeped through the layers of his jeans and her skirt, until she was nearly melting from the contact.

Talk—about anything—would be better than focusing on the hot waves of desire that were spiraling through her. "Have you heard from the adoptions people yet?"

"Nope." He drove with his right hand on top of the steering wheel, his left elbow resting on the windowsill. In profile, he was striking, a firm jaw, proud nose, and dark brown lashes so long any woman would kill for them.

"I've arranged for Judge Aldridge to marry us in his chambers at five o'clock on Wednesday."

"Great." He didn't look all that pleased.

"If you'd rather we do something different—"

"I said it was fine, didn't I?"

"You don't have to snap at me." She was anxious enough all on her own.

His hand closed even more tightly around the steering wheel, and he drew a breath that raised his chest. "Sweet sugar-Annie, if you don't move your leg away from mine, my voice isn't the only thing that's going to snap."

"I can't. I'm mashed—" She looked down at their legs plastered side by side, and in the process noted the telltale bulge in his jeans. If she'd been nervous before, she was mortified now. And secretly thrilled. "I'm sorry—"

"It's all right. I'll live." Though his voice was so choked, he sounded like he might be strangling.

She moved her rear end as far to the right as she could, practically sitting in Bets's infant seat to get out of Reed's way. It didn't help her much. What she could no longer feel, she could certainly remember.

Despite her best efforts not to, she got a clear picture of what their wedding night would be like—hot, sweaty and very elemental.

For a moment it was all she could do to draw a breath.

THE COUNTY BUILDING was a jarring combination of concrete and Spanish motif. They found their way to the license bureau.

The couple waiting ahead of them looked so

young, Ann could have sworn some of her seventh-grade students were older. It made her feel ancient.

"How old are you?" she asked Reed. Though she knew he'd grown up in Mar del Oro, as she had, she couldn't remember them being in school together. Surely she would have noticed him, given her propensity for seeking out bad boys.

"Twenty-seven." He expertly balanced Bets on his shoulder.

"I'm thirty." That meant she'd been well ahead of him in school and explained why she hadn't remembered him.

His lips twitched. "Fortunately, I'm partial to older women."

She would have hit him with the nearest pillow for calling her *older,* but before she could find one in the austere office, the couple ahead of them had gotten their license and moved away, sucking embarrassingly loud kisses as they went. Ann rolled her eyes. That wasn't her style. Never had been. Until now. And she doubted Reed would even acknowledge the importance of this moment when they were all done with the lengthy forms.

The clerk, who was barely tall enough to be seen above the counter, gushed, "I'm so pleased when couples decide to get married, however belatedly. Of course, in my day, we tied the knot before there was a baby. Better late than never, I always say."

Ann wanted to deny her maternity. "I'm not—"

"We wanted to make sure we were right for each other," Reed said smoothly. "Could you just give us whatever forms are necessary?"

The clerk looked at him askance, her narrow face like a hatchet set on axing weddings that shouldn't take place. Ann felt guilty for agreeing to a marriage based on expediency instead of mutual love. But Reed needed her. His approval as Betina's adoptive parent depended upon him being married to a woman with impeccable references. More than that, Ann sensed he needed her in order to learn about unquestioning love. It was a theorem of the heart she intended to prove.

They didn't share much more conversation on the way back to Del Oro High than they had on the way to the county courthouse. Reed pulled up next to her Mustang, the headlights of his truck cutting through the twilight in the teachers' parking lot.

"You want me to pick you up Wednesday here at school or at your house?" he asked.

"No," she said quickly. "I'll meet you at the courthouse."

He raised his brows.

"It's unlucky for the groom to see his bride on the wedding day before the ceremony."

"You're kidding, right?"

No, she wasn't. She needed all the luck she could get if she was going to make her marriage to Reed Drummond work. If bowing to a superstitious notion helped, she'd take every advantage she could. "I'll meet you there," she reiterated.

INSTEAD OF GOING directly home, Ann drove into town to Dora's Miniature World. Dora was in the process of closing the shop when Ann arrived.

She looked up from counting her cash receipts. "Hi, hon, how's it going?"

"The past couple of days have been rather interesting."

"Hmm, wish I could say the same. Business has been a little slow." She picked up a stack of ten-dollar bills and began adding them to the pile of twenties, mouthing the increasing total amount.

"I'm getting married on Wednesday. I'd like you to come."

Dora's hands froze in mid-motion. She blinked and turned her head. "Darn it all, don't kid about things like that. You made me lose count."

"Five o'clock, Judge Aldridge's chambers."

"Oh, my God! My—" She lost all interest in her bookkeeping activities. Laughing, she rushed to Ann to give her a crushing hug. "I didn't even know you were seeing anyone."

"I haven't been. Not exactly."

Looking nonplussed by Ann's answer, Dora asked, "So who's the lucky man?"

"Reed Drummond, and don't you dare tell me I'm making a mistake."

"Of course I wouldn't..." Her heavy brows drew together. "Are you?"

"I don't know, Dora. I honestly don't know." Shifting her hair behind her shoulder, she told Dora about Reed and his baby, Betina. How determined he was to adopt the child. She waxed on at some length about his being a loner, no doubt a result of having been raised by an abusive father. And when she finally slowed down, Dora looked at her, shaking her head.

"Are you in love with him?"

Ann considered the question, making an effort to be as objective as possible. On a scale of one-to-ten, lust was way up there; so were her feelings for Betina. But love? At least a seven, she'd say.

"I certainly think it's worth my time to explore the possibility to its fullest," Ann said wryly, wishing she could be more confident of her own emotions.

"How does he feel about you?"

"He intends our marriage to be a temporary one, until he gets permanent custody of Betina." But he *wanted* her, and she hoped for now that would be enough…and that later his feelings would build into something far more potent.

"But you have a different idea about this arrangement being temporary." It wasn't a question. "Does he have any clue how stubborn you can be when you get set on something?"

"I don't think so."

Dora's smile broadened, and their eyes met in perfect understanding. "I wouldn't miss this for the world. He's not going to know what hit him."

Chapter Six

"I need you to sign this." Reed handed Ann several sheets of paper covered in bold handwriting that had to be his own. Very masculine. Very decisive.

They were waiting in the judge's chambers for him to complete his courtroom work for the day. Reed had on a white dress shirt and what looked to be brand-new jeans. Ann had the urge to straighten the knot of his tie but the lack of any real intimacy in their relationship made the gesture seem awkward. She was pleased he'd "spruced up" for the occasion, and in his way, he looked devastatingly handsome. Perhaps he wasn't taking this marriage as casually as she'd feared.

She'd chosen to wear a pale green silk dress with a flowing skirt for her wedding day, in part because she was confident she'd be able to get into Reed's truck after the ceremony without his assistance. She'd kept her jewelry simple, a string of pearls and matching earrings.

In contrast, Dora's dress was a summery print with a flattering scooped neckline and sheath skirt.

She'd been thoughtful enough to bring Ann a bouquet of spring flowers to carry. At the moment, however, she was tactfully cooing over Bets, who was responding with her own unintelligible babble.

"What is it?" Ann asked Reed, glancing at the papers.

"It's a prenuptial agreement. Basically it says what's mine is mine and what's yours is yours. When we get divorced, nobody owes anybody anything."

Nothing like planning for a dismal future, though perhaps she should have given the prospect of failure a little more thought herself. She had quite a bit to lose—beyond her heart. "Shouldn't we have an attorney look it over?"

"I took it nearly word for word out of a book I got at the library. It'll stand up in court."

She supposed it would. If nothing else, Reed was a very thorough man. It seemed unlikely he intended to do anything more than protect his ranch, which was entirely reasonable given his view that their marriage would be a temporary one.

Fully prepared to sign the document, she read it through until she came to the last paragraph.

Her head snapped up. "You're demanding full custody of Betina."

"You've got that damn straight."

Something tightened in her chest. Whatever had she been thinking? Of course Reed would want Betina. That was the whole object of this subterfuge. For him, Ann was only a means to an end. If they ended up separating, she'd have no say in the child's life. Not even visitation privileges. That prospect hurt more than she could have imagined possible, almost as much as the thought of losing Reed. With both of them, she'd have to find some way to protect her heart. That wouldn't be easy.

"Of course," she murmured. He wouldn't marry her if she didn't sign the agreement, then there'd be no chance at all for her to nurture whatever feelings he had for her into something truly lasting.

With a shaky hand and a stomach almost knotted in on itself, Ann signed the document. He took it from her without comment, folded it lengthwise and stuffed it into his hip pocket.

A muscle twitched in his jaw. "All we need now is the judge."

Ann needed much more than that—like six months of courtship or a friendly word. She wasn't going to get either of those things. And it was too late to ask.

The judge breezed into the room, shedding his black robe as he did. His full head of gray hair made him look distinguished; regular games of golf had tanned his face, making him appear athletic. "Are we all set to go?"

"We are, your honor," Reed said.

The judge checked with Ann. "Aren't your parents coming?"

A wall clock with golf clubs for hands read five-fifteen. If her parents were coming, they'd have been here by now. Ann tried not to feel the disappointment too keenly. "No, sir."

For a moment, Judge Aldridge looked taken

aback but quickly recovered. "You're well beyond the age of consent. Let's do it, shall we?"

He lured a uniformed marshal into his chambers to serve as best man and the second witness, along with Dora as maid of honor, and proceeded with the ceremony.

As far as Ann was concerned, the words were pretty much a blur but when the judge asked about rings, she produced a gold band for Reed.

His eyebrows lifted and he gave her a wry smile. "You trying to hog-tie me, sweet sugar? You don't have to do that. The judge here is making it official."

"It'll be more convincing to the adoptions people if you have a ring," she told him quietly before he could refuse to accept the token of her unspoken love. It would also mark him as her husband, just as she became his wife when, in return, he slipped a similar gold band on her finger.

He spoke his vows in an even, steady voice; hers quavered.

The whole thing was over too soon.

"You may kiss the bride."

He hesitated for the length of a painful heartbeat, his gaze sweeping over her with possessiveness and blatant lust. Then his lips covered hers, oh so lightly. It was a whisper of a kiss, less than she'd expected, no more than a promise. She wanted more; she wanted less. A tangle of nerves crowded in her throat.

The judge congratulated Reed.

Pleasure, hope and friendship filling her eyes,

Dora hugged Ann. "Say, you two, why don't I baby-sit Bets for you tonight. So you can have some time alone."

"The baby's fine with us." Reed picked up his daughter and the diaper bag.

"Here, I'll take that," Ann offered. He handed over the bag.

"At least let me take your picture," Dora insisted.

Reed tried to protest, but Dora ignored him, producing an instant camera and snapping their picture. Ann's forced smile felt as if it had been carved out of plaster. She wondered if Reed had bothered to smile at all.

Moments later, as they left the courthouse, Reed's hand palmed the small of her back in a gesture that heated through her dress as though he had branded her his wife. His property.

"Where's your car?" he asked.

"Over there." She indicated a spot a couple of rows over in the nearly empty parking lot. "I just have to get my overnight case and my dress for tomorrow. Dora's going to drive my car back to town and leave it in the school parking lot. You'll have to drive me in in the morning."

"That'll be fine."

"I'll pick up more of my clothes from home tomorrow." Though they were acting like two strangers planning to be college roommates, the undercurrent of sexual chemistry was volatile. Ann suspected the lessons he could teach her wouldn't be found in any ordinary textbook.

Dora had trailed them out of the building. Together they retrieved Ann's small case and light hanging bag, transferring them to Reed's truck.

"He's one potent cowboy," Dora whispered.

"Yes, I know."

"I'd say if this thing between you two works out, you're going to have your hands full."

A smile curled Ann's lips ever so slightly. "That's not all I intend to have full." She wanted her heart filled with his love, too.

ANN WANDERED around Reed's house in a half dream. Bets had fallen asleep in the truck on the way home, and Reed had put her down in her crib. Then he'd changed clothes and gone out to do his evening chores, an excited Arnold at his side. Ann had changed, too, into slacks and comfortable shoes, though she kept popping in to check on Betina, half hoping the baby would wake so she'd have a chance to hold her a while.

In the meanwhile, Ann explored what was to be her new home—however temporarily.

Granted the house didn't have much going for it now but if you believed in *location-location-location* being the key value of any real estate, then its potential was limitless. Every window had a view of rolling hills and valleys or the distant ocean. With a bit of remodeling, some newer furniture and a lot of paint, the place could be a storybook home. Just as she'd fallen for Reed so quickly, she was in love with his home now as well.

From all she'd seen, she was pretty sure Reed didn't have much money. She didn't care. Some day this would be one of the most prosperous ranches along the central California coast. Reed would see to that.

To keep herself occupied, she rooted out some ground meat in the refrigerator and found buns to make hamburgers for dinner. Something less than a gourmet feast for a wedding night but she doubted her nervous stomach would care. Eating was among the very last things on her mind at the moment.

REED CAME INTO the house through the back door and the mudroom. As soon as he reached the kitchen, he stopped dead in his tracks.

In that dress she'd worn for their brief wedding ceremony, she'd looked good enough to eat—as sweet and silky as one of those fancy crème-de-menthe pies.

Even now, dressed more casually, she still looked too good, too classy to be standing at the stove in his house, flipping burgers. Not only was she the sexiest woman he'd ever seen, in an understated way, she dripped with cool sophistication. Not the kind of woman he was used to dealing with. Not the kind of woman he deserved.

But the kind of woman he wanted.

His wife. However temporarily. And he was damn well going to take advantage of whatever she was willing to give for as long as he could—at least until Bets was his.

In the judge's chambers he'd kept his cool. As much as he'd wanted to kiss her long and deep and hot after the old guy had pronounced them man and wife, he'd managed to stay in control. One kiss like the one he'd wanted to give her, and he would have lost it. The judge probably wouldn't have been all that impressed if he'd shoved his fancy pen set and spotless blotter off his mahogany desk and taken sweet sugar-Annie right there on top of it.

Annie probably wouldn't have been all that pleased either, he considered with a grin.

He stepped into the room. "I thought after you got a good look at the place you'd take off."

She started, nearly knocking the frying pan off the stove. "I don't quit anything I start that easily, Reed. Given enough time, you'll learn that about me."

Her sugarcoated voice wrapped itself around a hard core of steel. What the hell was she up to? She knew this was going to be a short gig, a temporary arrangement. That's what he'd offered and that's what she had agreed to.

He washed up at the sink while she served the burgers and fries. He'd just sat down and taken a single bite when the baby cried. He shoved back his chair.

"Let me get her," Ann offered. "You eat your dinner."

"You've got to be hungry, too."

"Not really."

He eyed her speculatively. "She'll need changing, and then she'll need a bottle."

"I understand thousands of women manage to do that every day. I think I can handle it."

"If you're sure."

"Look at it this way, Reed. What will the adoption people think if I can't change a diaper or feed the baby a bottle? They'd hardly nominate me for Adoptive Mother of the Year."

She had him there. If they were going to make their joke of a marriage look real, Ann had to be involved with caring for the baby. Bets would have to get used to Ann holding her, feeding her. Reed wasn't sure he liked the idea of sharing her, but then he realized if he'd found a housekeeper the net result would have been the same. Except he wouldn't be hoping to sleep with the housekeeper—and his jeans wouldn't be feeling about two sizes too small.

By the time Ann returned with Bets in her arms, Reed had finished off one burger and was helping himself to a second one from the stove. She went to the refrigerator just like she knew what she was doing and retrieved a bottle of formula he'd made up that morning.

"How long do I zap it in the microwave?" she asked.

"Thirty seconds usually does it."

He went back to the table, nibbled on the cold fries from his plate and watched Ann move with easy grace around his kitchen. Her slacks curved sleekly over her butt, right where he wanted to place his hand. The soft flare of her hips made him think of a woman made for making babies, and he imagined her body thickening with his baby growing inside.

Bad idea, he told himself, turning his attention to his burger. No reason to complicate his life by getting her pregnant. She wasn't going to stick around. That wasn't part of the deal.

She settled down in the chair opposite him, Bets in the crook of her arm. A soft, maternal smile played at the corners of her lips as the baby eagerly accepted the bottle from her. The two of them looked so contented, so damn natural together, Reed felt left out. He didn't want to think of Ann as Bets's mother. That would mean something permanent that simply wasn't in the cards for him...or her.

He tamped down an unexpected wave of regret. "Do you want me to show you how to make up the formula for her?" he asked.

She lifted her head. To Reed's surprise, tears sheened her eyes, making them look like polished emeralds. "Yes, I'd like that. Thank you. Thank you for letting me feed her."

Her wrenching emotion jolted him and caught him off guard. Down deep, he wanted to be on the receiving end of that much love. It wasn't likely to happen. Not in this lifetime.

When Bets finished her bottle, Ann burped her and continued to play with the baby in her lap. She couldn't get enough of touching her, feeling the softness of her skin, watching her random movements, smelling her baby scent of talcum powder and milk. It was like finally holding a Christmas present she'd been sure she'd never get—and was still afraid she'd lose. *Don't get too close,* she cautioned herself even as she recognized the warning came too late.

"How did you learn to take care of a baby so quickly?" she asked, glancing across the table at

Reed. "It can't have been easy, suddenly finding yourself a father."

"The pediatrician in Forth Worth where Bets was born started me off. The rest I picked up from books I got at the library."

She arched her brows in surprise. "Sounds like you're a frequent library patron."

"Old habit. When I was growing up we didn't have money for books, not that my old man would have let me buy them if we had. So I hung out at the library, then hid the ones I brought home under the bed." He stood and carried the plates to the counter. "Mrs. Thurgood used to waive the fines if I messed up and brought the books back overdue."

"I remember her. She was ancient when I was in first grade. The town finally got her to retire a couple of years ago, on her eightieth birthday. Everybody made a big deal of it."

He set Ann's uneaten hamburger aside and rinsed the plates. "I'm sorry I wasn't here to help her celebrate."

"If you were such a library hound... I got the impression from Mr. Dunlap that academics weren't your forte."

"Whenever my ol' man had a hangover, which was damn often, he kept me home to do the chores. That made it pretty hard to keep up in school."

But he wasn't stupid, Ann realized. Any man who went out of his way to learn from books had to be intelligent. She'd seen the keen alertness in his eyes from the beginning. She simply hadn't fully recognized how deep that intelligence went.

"Our talkative principal also suggested you were responsible for a lot of vandalism around the school."

Reed eyed her over his shoulder. "If Dunlap was talking about the night all those windows were broken, he's wrong. But other stuff?" He shrugged. "I wasn't exactly a perfect kid."

Ann had suspected that from the beginning. Oddly, that was a part of Reed's appeal.

He finished the dishes, leaving them to dry on a rack.

"Time for Bets to call it a night," he announced.

As she relinquished the baby to Reed, Ann's arms felt suddenly empty, as though she'd lost something near and dear to her. A sense of vulnerability swept over her. Nervously, she shifted the tips of her hair behind her shoulder. Very soon now Reed would claim his right to the next part of their bargain.

"I'll put her down, then take a shower," he said. "It won't take me long."

"How long will she sleep?"

"Till two or three." He gave her a slow, hungry look and a lazy, sexy smile that made her heart tumble in her chest. "Assuming you're still interested, we'll have plenty of time."

She understood what he was saying. He wanted her ready...and willing.

SHE WASN'T READY.

The scent of steam and soap billowed out of the bathroom when Reed appeared. He'd wrapped a towel around his waist; the ginger-brown swirls of hair on his broad chest looked crisp and clean, inviting a woman's touch. His bare skin was slightly flushed where it hadn't been tanned by the sun and invited a woman's kiss.

Ann's mouth went totally dry. She couldn't have uttered a word if her life had depended upon it. She was riveted to the spot, aware of the double bed in the room and how totally inadequate it would be for Reed, let alone for the two of them.

He arched his brows. "A cotton nightgown?"

Her nipples puckered under his intense scrutiny. "I didn't have time to shop for anything more…more…"

"Sexy," he provided.

Her throat tightened. "I'm sorry."

"Don't be." He strolled toward her in a loose-limbed way. "It's the kind of thing a man wants to take off."

She shot a glance toward the bed—*the totally inadequate bed.* "There's something I should mention."

His eyes narrowed. "If you've changed your mind—"

"No, it's not that. It's just…" She pursed her lips. Her heart was beating so hard, she suspected he could hear it from where he stood. "It's been a long time, is all."

"Yeah. It's been a while for me, too."

His admission eased her more than she might have expected. Perhaps she'd misjudged him as badly as the townspeople had. Though in this case she doubted it had been thirteen years since he'd made love to a woman. That record surely qualified her as a born-again virgin.

Stepping closer, he said, "Did you know you always do a flip thing with your hair when you get nervous?"

"I hadn't realized."

"Let me." He lifted her hair, shifting it behind her shoulders, and dipped his head to kiss her at the juncture of her neck. Gooseflesh sped down her spine, and somewhere low in her body, she clenched. "You smell good," he murmured against her throat. "Like a fresh-cut rose."

"You smell very—" *Male,* she'd meant to say. But her voice caught as he nibbled lightly on her shoulder with his teeth, then sucked to ease the slight tingling sensation. She tipped her head to give him free access for whatever he wanted to do.

Instinctively she palmed his chest. Not to push him away but to explore the broad expanse, eager to feel the warmth of his flesh and test the springy curls she'd so admired.

He took his time, kissing her neck and finally finding that sensitive spot below her ear. She wondered when he'd kiss her, really kiss her, and she groaned in frustration. "Reed, I want..."

"We've got lots of time."

He gave the same careful attention to her face, kissing her eyes closed, letting her feel the random touch of his lips everywhere but on her mouth. She pressed herself against him, rubbing like a cat demanding affection, hooking her arms around his neck. When he finally granted her mouth the pleasure of his lips, circling and dipping with his tongue, he began to fill that empty space inside her that had been vacant for a very long time.

She responded with gratitude and joy.

Their deepening kiss escalated quickly. Heat and passion waged a brief battle with restraint and won. Reed fell with her crossways onto the bed, his hands slipping under her nightgown, raising it above her hips. He skimmed his hand across her belly, then bared her breasts to his examination. The hot look in his eyes seared her. She gasped and pulled him to her.

This was the man she belonged with, the one she'd been waiting for all of her life. Her husband. Her lover. *Till death us do part.*

A prayer filled her chest. Let this be forever, she pleaded.

Incredible heat and need exploded in her as he laved her puckered nipples to hardened nubs. She writhed beneath him, arching her back. "Please..."

"Easy does it, sweet sugar-Annie." He tested her readiness with his finger, and her muscles closed around him.

From the drawer of the bedside table, he withdrew a foil packet. Her hand strayed to cover his as he sheathed himself, and then he was above her, entering her.

Her body, unused to stretching to accommodate such a primitive invasion, rebelled momentarily. He withdrew slightly, starting again. This time he slipped into her slick tightness with ease—filling her gloriously.

"Yes," she sighed, lifting her legs around him.

"Yes," he echoed, a hint of painful self-control in his voice.

He set up a rhythm that was both slow and demanding, arousing her with each insistent thrust, going deeper, taking her higher. Her breath coming hard, she arched to meet him.

She lost track of where her body ended and his began. She absorbed him, and he her. Two became one in an exquisite meeting of flesh.

A fine sheen of sweat dampened his back, and she writhed beneath him, her fingers digging into the contour of muscle and sinew. She felt herself peaking, the sensation a wave of rippling pleasure that rose from deep within her.

"Reed! Oh...I..."

"Let it go, sweet sugar. Let it go."

She did. There was no holding back. The force swept upward until she burst with it, and she cried out again, her legs tightening around him.

One more thrust and he groaned, too. Low and deep and filled with hunger.

LATER ANN FELT REED leave the bed in response to Bets's hungry cry. She missed the warmth of his big body spooned along her back and sleepily waited for his return.

As she had expected, Reed was an excellent lover. Tender and thorough. But in some deep recess of her mind, she felt something was wrong. He'd held back a part of himself.

When he returned, she snuggled against him. He held her but he didn't try to make love to her again.

A sharp sense of disappointment sliced through her chest. He'd eased his need for a woman with her but she hadn't yet come close to touching his heart.

Chapter Seven

Reed pulled his truck in next to Ann's car in the school parking lot.

She'd gotten up early enough to feed Bets her morning bottle and then had fixed him eggs and pancakes while he'd been out checking the stock. Hell, he couldn't remember the last time someone besides a hired cook for a cattle ranch or somebody in a greasy-spoon diner had made him breakfast. It wasn't something he ought to get used to. It wouldn't last.

As he got out of the truck, he prided himself on his self-control, only making love to her once last night. Not that he hadn't wanted to do a helluva lot more, particularly when she'd snuggled her sweet little rear end right up against his groin when he'd come back from giving Bets her bottle in the middle of the night. Damn! Sugar Annie had felt so good. So willing.

He broke out in a sweat just thinking about how good it had been making love to her, being inside her. That wasn't going to last, either. He kept telling himself if they only did it once a night, maybe he wouldn't miss her so much when she was gone.

He took her elbow as she got out of the truck. *Don't get too close,* an inner voice warned. Nobody you care about sticks around for long.

"I've gotta find a housekeeper to watch out for Bets during the day," he said. "I'm not getting my work done, taking care of her, too."

She glanced toward a big yellow school bus that had arrived. "I know a woman who does day care. She only lives a block or two from school. If she has an opening—"

"I'd rather keep Bets at home. She's not even six weeks yet."

"Yes, I suppose you're right." Students piled noisily out of the bus. "Let me think about it. There must be some grandmotherly type around who'd be interested."

His lips quirked. "When I was looking for a replacement for Lupe, everybody in town gave me the cold shoulder. No matter how ancient, they thought I was planning to seduce them. And with the young ones, I had their mothers on my case."

Standing on tiptoe, she kissed him right smack on the lips, then grinned. "I'll promise whoever's interested that I'll keep you in line. We'll find somebody."

He felt dumbstruck. He hadn't expected her to make their new relationship so obvious. Not on her turf at school with a couple of dozen kids getting an eyeful.

"I'll be home by about five or five-thirty," she said. "I'll stop to pick up something for dinner."

"Sure. If you want."

"I want," she said softly. Her eyes said dinner wasn't the only thing she had in mind.

His juices stirring in anticipation, he watched her walk through the front gate. She'd called his run-down ranch house *home*. She couldn't have meant that, not for the long term. She was only playing a part, setting herself up as a believable wife so when the adoptions people investigated, their marital act would ring true. He should feel grateful. And he wondered why their whole charade made him feel sick to his stomach.

"Ooo-eee, cowboy! Is she one hot mama or what?"

Reed whirled and grabbed Jason by the shirtfront, yanking him up on his toes. "Don't you ever say anything bad about that lady, you hear me?"

The kid's eyes widened. "Yeah, sure. I didn't mean nuthin'. Honest." His voice came out an octave higher than normal.

"You'll hear from me if you do, and it won't be pleasant." He eased his grip on the kid. "I'm thinking of hiring a ranch hand—part-time. I need somebody who's tough. You interested?" Put that way, Reed figured it was a challenge a kid with this much bluster couldn't pass up.

"Me?" His voice squeaked, but not with fear this time.

"What? You think I'm talkin' to the man in the

moon? You're the only one around, aren't you? You want a job or don't you?''

Shrugging out of Reed's grasp, Jason straightened his shirt and tried to look nonchalant. ''So how much are you paying?''

As if it mattered. Reed would have killed for a way to earn money of his own when he'd been Jason's age. ''Minimum wage. And don't give me some garbage about you being worth more than that.''

''No…well, I am, but heck, I'm between—''

''You'll have to get the okay from your foster parents.''

''They won't care.''

''How you planning to get to my place?''

''On my bike. I've got a bike.''

He was luckier than Reed had been at his age. ''It's uphill most of the way.''

Jason puffed up his chest. ''You just said you wanted somebody tough. I'll make it.''

Smothering a grin, Reed nodded. ''Okay. Tomorrow. Be there by three or I'll hire somebody else.'' He knew damn well the kid would bust his butt to be there on time and every day thereafter. He also knew if he'd waltzed up to a smart aleck like Jason and announced he was going to ''mentor'' him, the youngster would have given him a wide berth—or worse.

Reed intended to keep his part of the bargain with sugar-Annie. Then when they split, he wouldn't owe her anything. That seemed fair.

Once a night. That's all he'd allow himself. He

didn't dare make her a habit that would be too hard to break.

"Ms. FORRESTER, I really do think you should conduct yourself with more decorum in the school's parking lot."

Ann had barely gotten inside her classroom when Mr. Dunlap appeared at the door. "I beg your pardon?"

"Really, Ms. Forrester! Kissing that man in front of the children. Whatever will they think?"

"They'll think I was kissing my husband goodbye and that I'm looking forward to seeing him tonight at home."

If he'd been a bowling pin—and his shape was not unlike one—the school principal would have toppled over from the force of the curve ball she'd thrown him.

"You couldn't...I mean, Reed Drummond is—"

"My husband." She had no intention of keeping the news a secret. Under other circumstances, she would have been shouting the announcement from the nearest rooftop. "We were married yesterday."

Dunlap's mouth worked but for a moment he didn't utter a sound. Finally, he said, "I wonder if the PTA would have chosen you for the Teacher-of-the-Year Award if they had known."

"Whom I'm married to doesn't have any effect—" She stopped short. "They did?"

"Yes. I shouldn't have told you, of course. It was meant to be a surprise. The announcement won't be made until the meeting Thursday night, in time for a press release to the newspaper. There'll be a photo of you and story. But I was, well, shocked by your news."

A warm feeling rose in Ann's chest. Teacher-of-the-Year might not gain her so much as a free cup of coffee in town, but she was enormously pleased. She'd worked so hard, had strove to be the best teacher she could be, and the fact that someone else had noted her efforts was deeply satisfying. An announcement in the *Mar del Oro Press Enterprise*— the paper the locals fondly referred to as the MOPE—would be worth saving for those stressful days when her students stretched the limits of her patience.

"Thank you, Mr. Dunlap. I won't let on that I know."

"Yes, of course." He sputtered self-consciously. "Well, then, I guess I should offer my congratulations and best wishes, Ms. Forrester."

She suspected he intended those best wishes to be for her selection as an outstanding teacher, not for her marriage to Reed Drummond.

Another feeling swept through her then, one that made her giddy with a combination of happiness and trepidation. "I'm Mrs. Drummond, now, Mr. Dunlap. Perhaps you should get used to calling me by that name."

She proudly wrote her new name on the chalkboard as the students gathered in the classroom. By second period the entire school had heard the news. The girls were filled with giggles and admiration, the boys seemed surprised, almost as if she'd be-

trayed them. Her fellow teachers had a mixed reaction, as she discovered in the teachers' room during snack break.

"I had no idea you'd been seeing anyone,"
Marcy McCullough said. "Much less that you were
serious about that cowboy."

"It did happen rather quickly," Ann conceded,
pouring herself a cup of very black coffee. Getting
up at 5 a.m. certainly lengthened her morning.

"He's just the kind of man I warn my girls
against," Adrean Thumb cautioned sourly. A grandmother of three teenage girls, she was a shade over-
protective, perhaps rightly so since the youngsters
tended to be on the wild side. "I remember when
he was in school. I had him in eighth grade social
studies. A real hellion—"

"He's grown up now." And very nicely, in Ann's
view.

Before the break was over, she found herself
fielding questions about the baby and defending
Reed, all the while trying not to give away too many
details about their relationship, or that it was intended to be temporary.

"We'll have to give you a shower," Marcy announced as they headed back to their respective
classrooms. "Goodness, we can do a combined
wedding and baby shower. That'll be such fun!"

"That's very sweet of you to offer." Stopping at
her classroom door, Ann touched Marcy's arm, halt-
ing her, too. "But let's wait a while. Reed and I are
still..." *Strangers.* "...getting to know each other.

We're making so many changes, so suddenly, I don't even know what I'll need.''

"Well, if you say so. But I know all the teachers will want to—''

The bell sounded.

"We'll talk later,'' Ann assured her, slipping the key into the classroom door. She could hardly approve of her friends going to all the trouble and expense of a shower when she wasn't sure the marriage would actually last. Oh, she hoped Reed would come around to wanting their arrangement to be permanent. But she couldn't count on it.

"Say,'' Marcy said, before she could get away. "I saw you shopping in San Luis Obispo on Saturday, but I guess you didn't see me. I called to you—''

"Sorry, it wasn't me.'' Ann stood aside to let the students file into the room. "I was busy gardening Saturday.'' And receiving the first and only marriage proposal of her life.

Marcy's expression clouded. "Funny, I could have sworn...'' She shrugged. "Oh, well, I'll see you later.'' Turning, she entered her own classroom, admonishing one of her students to get down off the table.

Later that afternoon when Ann stopped by her house to pick up her clothes, she paused beside the fireplace mantel. Smiling, she pressed a kiss to her fingertips then rested them on the miniature cowboy mounted on his horse.

"You aren't going to get rid of me as easily as

you think, Mr. Dream Man. Being tenacious is one of my finest attributes.''

She packed the miniature in its original box and took it with her, managing not to dwell on the disappointment that there hadn't been a message from her parents on her answering machine. After a hurried stop at the grocery store, she headed up the hill to the ranch. *To her new home.*

Reed wasn't in sight when she got there, nor was Bets, though the pickup was parked out front. Ann put the groceries away and hung her clothes in the closet. There was plenty of room. Reed's limited wardrobe didn't exactly make a fashion statement, but they smelled of him, a rich masculine scent that somehow overpowered the scent of laundry powder. Or perhaps it was just that the room, with its unmade bed, still held the lingering musky perfume of their sex.

She changed into jeans, and wearing a light jacket, went in search of Reed.

Instead, Arnold found her.

''Where is he, boy?'' She gave the dog a vigorous pet and scratched him behind his ears. In return, Arnold gave her monstrously juicy licks on her face, and she laughed. Since she'd been a little girl, she'd wanted a dog. Her parents had demurred. Living alone in her own house, Ann had felt it unfair to leave an animal all by himself while she worked. Chalk another one up for the joys of matrimony, she thought with a grin.

Arnold, his tail wagging, led her across the rolling hills to a spot where Reed was sitting on a low, flat rock looking out toward the ocean and the approaching evening fog. He had Bets with him, cuddled against his chest in her sling. From the dejected slump of his shoulders, Ann got the terrible feeling something was wrong. Then she noticed an official-looking envelope on the ground beside him.

"Did you hear from the adoptions people?"

He didn't look in her direction. "Nope. That shoe hasn't dropped yet."

Worried, she crouched down beside him. "What is it? What's wrong?" Impulsively, she palmed his cheek, and he turned away.

"The bank. They're cancelling my line of credit and calling in what I owe."

He spoke so stoically, it took Ann a moment to overcome the hurt of his rejection and grasp the meaning of his words. "They're foreclosing?"

"Same as. I used a line of credit to start the herd and replace some of the broken equipment around here. I had to use the land as collateral."

"You could sell off the cattle—"

"And do what for income? Come winter, I'll be grazing other people's beef to fatten 'em up and getting rent money, but if I don't have a herd of my own this place will never show a profit. And if I lose the land..." He shrugged. "I'll be back to being a hired hand. Bunkhouses aren't exactly designed for a family man."

Ann realized he wasn't only worried about his ranch but having a place to raise his daughter, too. "You had everything planned, didn't you?"

"It looked good on paper."

How could a bank have foreclosed so quickly? So cruelly? He'd only been back in the area for a few months. They hadn't even given him a chance to prove he could make it as a rancher.

A possible reason came to her, so heartless it stunned her. "Which bank is carrying your loan?" she asked, almost certain what his answer would be.

"The one in town, Central Bank of California."

Anger drove her to her feet, startling Arnold from his nap and making Reed look up sharply.

"It's my father. He's done this to you. To *us*. Because he disapproved of my marrying you."

"What's your father got to do with the bank?"

"He's retired now but he's still on the board. The president emeritus, and you can damn well bet he's got plenty of influence when it comes to making loans. And calling them in."

Reed's eyes narrowed, and he stood, automatically giving extra support to the baby cradled in his arms. "He must love you very much," he said tautly.

"He's interfering with *my* business, is what he's doing. And I'm not going to let him destroy everything you've worked for—for yourself and for Betina." She planted her fist on her hip. "I'm going to talk to him first thing—"

"Leave it be. I can fight my own battles."

"But this one is *my* fault. If I hadn't married you—"

"I might not be able to adopt Bets."

"You still might not be allowed to if you don't have a place to raise her."

"You think I don't know that?" His words sliced through the evening air as he turned to stride across the hills toward the house.

Ann had to half run to keep up. Lord, he'd married her because she had the spotless reputation he thought he needed to make things all right with the adoptions people. Now it might not be enough. "How much time did they give you?"

"Ten days."

"I have some money, Reed—"

"No."

"Be reasonable. You don't want to lose the ranch. I don't want you to. We're married, for God's sake."

"It's my problem, sugar. I'll work it out."

Stubborn, pigheaded...man!

She threw up her arms in dismay. What did he think—that she was a tree stump that he could simply walk around? Married couples were supposed to share the burdens, not go their separate ways. And fathers were supposed to let their grown daughters live their own lives without interference.

She fumed all the way back to the house. In the kitchen, she slammed the dishes around while she fixed dinner, not sure whether she was more furious with her father or her husband.

Meanwhile Reed gave Bets her bottle. While they ate the chicken stir-fry she'd fixed, the baby played in her infant chair, trying to stick her fingers in her mouth, her big brown eyes alert to any movement in the room. There wasn't much talking between the newlyweds. Reed helped himself to a second portion, finishing the rice right from the pan. It occurred to Ann she'd have to plan bigger meals and double her shopping list. A man who worked on the land needed more nourishment than she'd realized.

"Did you have a chance to check on baby-sitters?" he asked as he carried his empty plate to the counter.

"Oh, darn. It slipped my mind. It was kind of a crazy day." And she'd spent a lot of it fending off probing questions about her sudden marriage and defending the man she'd chosen to marry. "I'm sorry. I'll do it tomorrow."

"Good. I've got some fencing I've gotta replace on the north side. It's hard with Bets."

Her curiosity getting the better of her, she asked, "How many acres do you own?"

"Just shy of a thousand."

"Good heavens! That's...amazing. To cover the loan, couldn't you sell off—"

"A ranch any smaller wouldn't be economically feasible. The land can't graze enough animals per acre to make it pay, assuming normal rainfall."

He'd probably gotten that from a library book, she thought as she finished her own meal. A thoughtful man like Reed would have the figures down to the number of eyelashes on a gnat. She wished her math students were that careful about the details. What a joy Reed would have been in a classroom—*if* he'd been allowed to attend school regularly.

They cleaned up the kitchen together. She could almost feel his worry, heavy and toxic in the air. She didn't want them to end the evening this way, the strain of his financial troubles keeping them apart.

He let Ann put Bets to bed while he showered.

Ann jumped at the opportunity to steal a few moments alone with Bets. Every time she came near the baby, she ached to cuddle her for fear she'd never have another chance. If her unconventional marriage to Reed failed, she'd lose Bets, too. She desperately didn't want that to happen. She'd already lost one child—along with a piece of her heart. She might never recover from the blow of losing another child she loved.

Leaning over a freshly diapered Bets, Ann placed tiny kisses on the baby's bare tummy. "Your daddy's a proud man, little Betina. Too proud for his own good."

The baby seemed to agree, blowing a derisive bubble. Unfortunately, Ann didn't know what to do about Reed's pride. It wasn't a personality flaw she particularly wanted to change. She just wished Reed wouldn't shut her out. There had to be some way she could help him.

When she'd finished putting Bets down, she found Reed in the living room, his hair damp from his shower, his shirt hanging open in the way that invited a woman's gaze to linger on the breadth of his chest. He'd left his jeans unsnapped, and that gave her other ideas as well. He was standing by the big native-rock fireplace, the dramatic focal point of the room. She was looking forward to sitting in front of a cozy fire with him this winter and maybe even making love in the firelight. If their marriage lasted that long.

"What's this thing on the mantel?"

"It's a Dream Man miniature from Dora's shop."

He cocked an eyebrow. "Of a cowboy and his mutt?"

"I prefer to call him Arnold."

His eyes narrowing, he gave her an odd look and shook his head incredulously. "That's your idea of a dream man?"

"Everyone needs some sort of a dream."

"There's only one thing I've been dreaming about lately." He extended his hand. "It's time for us to hit the sack, sweet sugar."

As invitations went, it was the best one she'd had all day. She'd been afraid he might not offer, but there was no doubt what he intended. And in spite of their disagreement and the way he kept locking her out, she was eager for them to make love. In bed she'd be able to show him just how much she cared even if he couldn't, or wouldn't, yet accept the depth of her feelings. Or reciprocate them.

He'd straightened the bed that she hadn't gotten around to making that morning and had pulled back the covers and fluffed the pillows. So inviting. So tempting.

Almost as self-conscious as she had been the first time, she turned away to unbutton her blouse. Slipping her top off, she dropped it along with her bra on a chair in the corner. She toed her shoes off and pulled her jeans down so she could step out of them. The cool night air raised chills on her flesh before

PLAY BANGO!

AND GET THREE FREE GIFTS!

It looks like BINGO, it plays like BINGO but it's FREE

HOW TO PLAY:

1. With a coin, scratch the Caller Card to reveal your 5 lucky numbers and see that they match your Bango Card. Then check the claim chart to discover what we have for you — FREE BOOKS and a FREE GIFT. All yours, all free!

2. Send back the Bango card and you'll receive 2 brand-new Harlequin American Romance® novels. These books have a cover price of $3.99 each in the U.S. and $4.50 each in Canada, but they are yours to keep absolutely free.

3. There's no catch. You're under no obligation to buy anything. We charge nothing — ZERO — for your first shipment. And you don't have to make any minimum number of purchases — not even one!

4. The fact is, thousands of readers enjoy receiving books by mail from the Harlequin Reader Service® months before they are available in stores. They like the convenience of home delivery and they love our discount prices!

5. We hope that after receiving your free books you'll want to remain a subscriber. But the choice is yours — to continue or cancel, any time at all! So why not take us up on our invitation, with no risk of any kind. You'll be glad you did!

YOURS FREE!
This exciting mystery gift is yours free when you play BANGO!

The Harlequin Reader Service® — Here's how it works:

Accepting free books places you under no obligation to buy anything. You may keep the books and gift and return the shipping statement marked "cancel." If you do not cancel, about a month later we'll send you 4 additional novels and bill you just $3.34 each in the U.S., or $3.71 each in Canada, plus 25¢ delivery per book and applicable taxes if any.* That's the complete price — and compared to the cover price of $3.99 in the U.S. and $4.50 in Canada — it's quite a bargain! You may cancel at any time, but if you choose to continue, every month we'll send you 4 more books, which you may either purchase at the discount price or return to us and cancel your subscription.

*Terms and prices subject to change without notice. Sales tax applicable in N.Y. Canadian residents will be charged applicable provincial taxes and GST.

If offer card is missing write to: Harlequin Reader Service, 3010 Walden Ave., P.O. Box 1867, Buffalo, NY 14240-1867

BUSINESS REPLY MAIL
FIRST-CLASS MAIL   PERMIT NO. 717   BUFFALO, NY

POSTAGE WILL BE PAID BY ADDRESSEE

HARLEQUIN READER SERVICE
3010 WALDEN AVE
PO BOX 1867
BUFFALO NY 14240-9952

NO POSTAGE
NECESSARY
IF MAILED
IN THE
UNITED STATES

she could put on the nightgown she'd left draped on the back of the chair.

"Leave it off," he ordered in a voice that was as soft as a caress.

Turning, she discovered he'd shed his clothes, too. Though she'd seen him naked last night, or nearly so, he still took her breath away. Or perhaps she'd been too busy absorbing a thousand other experiences, the tactile feel of him, the newness of it all, to admire him as thoroughly as he deserved. Now, with a leisurely chance to study Reed, she found him to be a magnificent specimen of masculinity. His broad shoulders tapered to lean hips, and there wasn't an extra ounce of fat on him. Resilient male flesh stretched over taut muscle and sinew.

He was male perfection, a sculptor's model. And he was fully aroused. Little wonder her body had been unable at first to accept his penetration, now that she'd gotten a good look at him.

She licked her lips and swallowed hard. With a dark gleam in his eyes, he watched her every movement. No man had ever looked at her with such intensity. It made her heart stumble, and she ached with the need to see more than lust in those burnished-bronze eyes of his.

Hurriedly, she slid into bed, pulling the blanket up to cover herself.

"Too late. I've already peeked." The corners of his mouth curved as he got into bed beside her. His muscular arm tugged her closer. "No need for you to hide from me, sugar."

"I wasn't hiding. Not exactly."

"Second-time jitters?"

"Something like that."

"Funny. I don't feel nervous at all."

Indeed, he seemed to have all the confidence in the world. With journeyman-like skill, he went about arousing her. All of her erogenous zones that he'd discovered the prior evening, he revisited with equal attention now. As she writhed beneath his ministrations, he kissed her in ways she'd never known, in places she'd never realized could be so sensitive.

"Reed…" His name escaped in a sob.

"I hear you, sugar-Annie."

He lifted her hips and slid into her. She welcomed him more easily this time, her body knowing his in intimate detail. Already on the brink, she spun out of control, sobbing his name again and again, digging her fingers into the muscles of his back as if there was a way to bring him even closer.

Only later, when he'd gathered her in his arms and she was drifting toward sleep did she sense he'd still held something of himself back. How could he do that, she wondered, when she'd been so lost in the magic of their coming together?

By morning she knew she would have to take drastic action if she had any hope of breaking through the barriers he'd created. And if Reed was worth fighting for, so was his ranch.

Immediately after school, she headed into town, to the Mar del Oro branch of the Central Bank of California.

She spotted David Emery Curtis III sitting behind

the same desk where her father had once reigned supreme. She used to love visiting her daddy here at the bank. He'd seemed so important, like a king with his minions ready to do his bidding. With the tellers fussing over her, Ann had been proud to be Richard Forrester's little girl.

Now she wasn't proud at all. Now she was madder than hell.

Chapter Eight

David rose in greeting. "Good afternoon, Ann. This is a pleasant surprise."

It wouldn't be if she dumped the vase of flowers decorating his desk into his lap. Which she was sorely tempted to do if he'd been the one to call in Reed's loan.

"I'd like to discuss a foreclosure the bank is planning."

His expression barely changed as he gestured for her to take the upholstered chair in front of his desk. In that regard, David reminded her of Reed—a man who was totally, frustratingly in control at all times.

"Are you interested in purchasing the property?" he asked with the same mild expression.

"Not likely. I already own it, in a manner of speaking." Though the prenuptial agreement she'd signed would mean she'd have no part of the ranch if she and Reed divorced. "I'm referring to Reed Drummond's place."

The hint of a blush darkened David's complexion, and he removed his glasses, polishing them vigorously with a clean, white handkerchief. "Yes, I understand best wishes are in order on your wedding. Last week when we dined with your parents, I was unaware you were...involved with anyone."

"I wasn't then. I am now, and I want to know exactly who ordered Reed's loan called in."

He replaced his glasses, adjusting them behind his ears with great care. "As you might imagine, I haven't yet had an opportunity to learn the details of all of the properties in which we have an interest. If you'll allow me a moment, I'll—"

"You weren't the one who foreclosed?"

"Not personally, no."

A frown tugged at her forehead. "I was sure my father had ordered you to call the loan because I married Reed against his wishes."

"Mrs. Drummond...Ann," he corrected, leaning forward. "I make banking decisions based on the best interests of our depositors, not the concerns of a father about his grown daughter's marital status. However much I may respect your father's experience and position here at the bank, I reach my decisions independently, and I can assure you, Mr. Forrester made no effort to influence me in this case. Nor would I have allowed it."

Chalk one up for David's integrity, Ann thought, her anger dissipating somewhat. "If not you, then who?"

"Let me see if I can get to the bottom of this."

He left her sitting at his desk while he went off to consult with his staff. Ann waited impatiently. She knew one of the tellers working behind the counter. The girl had been in Ann's eighth-grade math class the first year she'd started teaching. Now the young woman was obviously pregnant. Somehow that made Ann feel both old and envious.

David returned some time later with a thick file folder. He took his seat opposite her.

"It seems there was a general review of our loan portfolio. Our senior loan officer in San Luis Obispo concluded the credit line we had extended to Mr. Drummond was not justified. Therefore, the bank, in effect, has withdrawn the loan."

"And just who is the senior loan officer?"

He flipped through several pages. "Roger Clarke signed the papers."

Ann grimaced. Mr. Clarke had been with the bank almost forever and was one of her father's golfing partners. She should have known Richard Forrester would ask this kind of a favor from his friend, not his protégé.

"Is there any way to reverse the decision?" she asked.

"I doubt it. I'd be happy to inquire, but from the looks of these numbers, the loan was problematic to begin with. Cancellation is not an unreasonable decision."

"It's unreasonable if it's your livelihood that's at stake," she said tautly, fingering the plain gold band on her ring finger. *And the man she loved at risk.* "Tell me, does the bank go away and leave Reed alone if the loan is paid off?"

"Yes, of course."

Drawing a deep breath, she decided on the only

course of action that was open to her—a decision that would very likely make Reed mad and her father furious. But she was damn well going to save Reed from his own misplaced pride even if it cost her the husband she loved.

"David, I have a substantial equity in a small house I own here in town, and I believe you'll find my credit rating is excellent. I'd like to pay off the loan on the Rocking D Ranch by taking out a second mortgage on my house. Can you arrange that for me?"

A slow, curving smile animated David's features, changing him from a solemn banker to a prototypical model for *GQ*. "I believe I regret more now than ever that I didn't act more quickly when we first met. Reed Drummond is a very lucky man indeed to have landed you as his wife."

HER RESOLVE STILL firmly in hand after filling out a raft of loan papers at the bank, Ann headed toward her house above the town. Living in two places at once had its drawbacks, and she'd decided she definitely needed her Crock-Pot and a decent frying pan. Making meals for a hungry man involved far more than oven-roasting a skinless chicken breast and munching fresh carrots, her usual choice for a quick dinner.

To Ann's surprise, her mother's Cadillac was parked outside her house.

Parking her own car in the drive, Ann rushed up onto the porch. Her mother met her with open arms.

"I took a chance you might stop by the house before you went home."

With a sense of relief, Ann hugged her mother. "Oh, Mom..." Tears threatened, and she swallowed them down.

"I'm so sorry I missed the wedding, dear. Sometimes I just don't know what gets into your father."

"Does he know you're here now?"

"No, but he certainly can't stop me from seeing my own daughter, now, can he?"

"I certainly hope not." She unlocked the front door and they went inside.

"How are you, dear?"

"I'm fine." Or she would be if Reed didn't throw her out as soon as he learned she'd paid off his loan.

Her mother gave her a curious look. "You didn't mention this young man of yours has a baby girl."

News in a small town like Mar del Oro spreads as fast as a rising tide on dry sand. "She's not his, exactly. Not yet, anyway. He's trying to adopt her."

"Is that why you married him? To help him adopt the baby?"

Eleanor Forrester was often more perceptive than she cared to let on. "That's why he *asked* me, Mother. I *married* Reed because I love him."

"I see." She followed Ann into the kitchen. "So you're an adoptive mother?"

Ann bent down to get her Crock-Pot out of a low cupboard. "I suppose my name will be on the forms." Though if she didn't convince Reed that their arrangement ought to be permanent, she'd lose Betina, too.

"Life can be very strange," her mother said with a distracted air. "It all seems to go in circles, doesn't it?"

Ann didn't know what to make of that comment, so she let it slide as she found her frying pan and tried to think of any other tools or utensils that would make her domestic life a little easier.

"I'd always hoped when you had babies of your own that I'd be a part of their lives. And here you are, already a mother, and I haven't even met your husband yet."

Thinking Reed would probably like spaghetti, Ann reached for a colander and stopped short. A *grandmotherly* woman was exactly what Betina needed for a baby-sitter. "Mom, how would you like to get better acquainted with both Reed and his daughter?"

"Why, I think that would be very nice, dear."

"What about Dad? Would he throw a fit?"

After Ann explained what she wanted, and her mother accepted the job of full-time grandmother and part-time sitter, Eleanor Forrester said, "Let me handle your father, dear. After thirty-eight years of marriage, I still have a few tricks up my sleeve. And I *never* should have let him keep us away from your wedding."

They smiled conspiratorially and hugged again.

Later, as Ann drove up to the ranch, she pondered the stubborn look that had come into her mother's eyes when she'd decided to challenge her husband's authority. Ann had always assumed she'd taken after her father in terms of her personality—except for that one short fling with rebellion—though she didn't resemble him physically. Nor did she look a great deal like her mother, except for the color of her eyes. But now she wondered if she'd actually inherited her sometimes bullheaded determination from the maternal side of the family.

She hadn't told her mother how her father had manipulated the bank into calling in Reed's loan, a totally unethical maneuver, in her mind. She saw no reason, for now, to add fodder to what was already likely to be a tense situation between her parents. And Reed really needed a baby-sitter. Her mother would be perfect.

AS SHE PULLED UP in front of the ranch house, she spotted Jason pushing a heavily loaded wheelbarrow from the barn down the hill toward a dumping area. Sweat dampened his hair and dirt streak his shirt. Arnold padded merrily along at his side, his loyalty at least momentarily focused on the boy.

In contrast to the youngster who was working so hard, Reed was leaning indolently against the post on the front porch. His Stetson was tipped to the back of his head, his smile satisfied.

She got out of the car and popped the trunk. "What's going on?" she asked as she carried the Crock-Pot up the steps.

"That's my new hired hand. Part-time. Whaddaya think?" He looked very pleased with himself.

"Hired?"

"Sure. He's been busting his buns for five bucks an hour since he got here after school."

"I thought you were going to *mentor* him, not encourage him to get a job."

"That's exactly what I'm doing—mentoring. There's no more impressive lesson I could teach him than putting him to work. Nothing like mucking out a few horse stalls and hauling the manure away to figure out an education's a damn good idea."

Ann felt a new wave of admiration for Reed, and an ache of love filled her chest. He had indeed "been there, done that" and had learned his lessons in the hard school of experience. If anyone could turn Jason around, it would be Reed.

"I've been thinking," he went on in a pensive mood. "If I can figure out how to keep this place afloat, I need to get a couple more horses. That way Jason could help me move the stock, and someday I could teach Bets to ride."

"Has anyone mentioned lately that you're a good man, Reed Drummond?"

He cocked a questioning brow. "Not lately."

"And a good daddy, too." Unable to resist, she placed her hand on his arm. The heat of his skin seeped through the blue chambray fabric. "It's too bad Jason wasn't lucky enough to land a father like you."

His lips twitched. "Right at the moment I think the kid would run hell-bent-for-leather if anybody suggested that idea."

"Then that would be his loss." Laughing, she squeezed his arm. "Where's Bets, by the way?"

"Sleeping. She's due to wake up pretty soon."

He covered Ann's hand with his, idly smoothing his thumb over her polished thumbnail.

His gentle touch gave her a shiver of pleasure. "I think I've got our baby-sitting problem solved."

"Oh, yeah? Who'd you get?"

"My mother."

"You think that's a good idea?" His expression hardened. "After your old man set up this bank fore-closure business, I don't think I want any help from—"

"She's eager to play grandma, and she certainly has enough free time to help out. I think it will be good for her. Besides, most women who do day care would rather sit at their own homes instead of coming here."

"I don't know," he said doubtfully. "How's she going to feel about Bets after you and me split up?"

Pain replaced all the warm feelings that had filled Ann's chest, and she could barely draw a breath as she withdrew her hand. "Why don't we take this one step at a time? For now, Mom's the best baby-sitter I can come up with." Before he could see the hurt welling in her eyes, Ann carried the Crock-Pot into the house.

Reed straightened as the screen door closed behind him. He was being sucked into Ann's world like a stray mustang that got trapped in quicksand. She was too easy to be around, too soft to hold and touch when he knew damn well it wouldn't last. She'd suckered him into mentoring a scrawny kid, who was working so hard to prove himself his muscles would ache for a month. Now she'd gotten her mother involved in taking care of Bets.

Reed didn't like it. He didn't want to owe Ann or her family anything, particularly when her old man was trying to run him out of town.

All he'd wanted was to raise Bets like her mom had asked him to. For the rest of it, he just wanted to be left alone. Alone like he'd been all of his life. He was used to it.

"Hey, Mr. Drummond, I got that muck dumped." Jason's arms hung limply at his sides and he looked like he might topple over if a strong breeze came along. "What's next?" He breathed heavily.

"Looks like it's time for you to go on home."

The kid nodded.

"You coming back tomorrow?"

"When you gonna pay me?"

"End of the week. *If* you stick it out."

"I'll be here," he said grimly.

"Thought we might start putting new shingles on the barn roof tomorrow. Place leaks like a sieve when it rains."

"The roof?" His voice cracked as he shot a glance to the top of the sharply peaked structure.

"You scared of heights?"

He visibly swallowed. "Naw. Only sissies are afraid of stuff like that."

"You'll get over it." He mussed the kid's damp, sweaty hair. Yeah, Ann was right—the kid needed a decent father but Reed wasn't about to volunteer for the job. His plate was already plenty full. "Get on home now, and don't go too fast going down that hill. I don't want to have to mop you up with a blotter 'cause you couldn't make one of those curves.''

Jason shrugged out of reach, just as Reed would have as a kid. Trust didn't come easily to either one of them. Some lessons were hard to forget.

After the boy left, Reed checked that Fiero had been properly bedded down for the night. Then he turned off the light and stood outside, staring off over the hills toward the distant ocean. In spite of his troubles, the view soothed him. He'd save his land, his ranch—no matter the cost.

When he went inside, he found Ann fixing dinner. Her briefcase, which was overflowing with papers, was open on the kitchen table. He suddenly realized she'd been working all day, and given their wedding and erratic schedule the past couple of days, she was probably behind on her own work.

''Can I help fix dinner?'' he offered as he washed up.

''I've just about got everything ready. Pork chops, barbecue beans and a salad. Hope that's okay.''

''Sounds great.'' Better than great, considering he usually fixed himself a sandwich for supper. ''After dinner, I'll clean up while you do your schoolwork, if you want.''

''Thanks.'' Ann turned the meat in the skillet, and it sizzled, sending up a cloud of steam. Her stomach knotted on the thought of breaking the news to Reed that his loan was as good as paid off. Most men would be pleased to think their wife had enough assets to solve the problem. In Reed's case, she doubted that would be his reaction.

The question then was whether she ought to spoil their dinner with the fight that was likely to come. Unfortunately, procrastination was not her way. Since he'd already reminded her once tonight that he was still planning for their divorce, she had little to lose.

"I stopped by the bank today," she said casually as she set the salad on the table. "What kind of dressing do you like? I bought Italian and blue cheese."

"What did you do at the bank?"

"I arranged to pay off the loan on your ranch."

The room wouldn't have gone any quieter if a sudden plague had struck the earth, silencing every living being. The chops continued to sizzle in the pan, the beans bubbled to a low simmer. Reed didn't move.

"You what?" he asked. The tension in his voice was as taut as a guy wire strung between two mountain peaks.

"I have quite a bit of equity in my house. Or I had until I talked with the bank manager. I've arranged to take out a second mortgage and pay off your loan with the money."

"No."

"The proper response isn't *no*, it's thank you." Still assuming a casual attitude, in spite of the turmoil she was feeling, Ann stirred the beans.

Reed's hand closed around her arm, and he took the spoon away from her, turning her to face him.

His features were drawn into a fierce expression, his eyes dark. "I don't want you paying off the loan. I don't want your interference in my life or your money. Is that clear?"

"Don't be ridiculous, Reed. You can't lose the ranch. Where would you live? If my money can help, then—"

"If you pay off my loan, then you'll own a part of the ranch. Our prenuptial agreement wouldn't be worth the paper it's written on."

She yanked herself free of him. "So think of it as a loan. No interest. No due date. You won't be able to get better terms than those. Write up the damn agreement, if you're so pigheaded about it. I'll sign whatever you want."

"I don't need your money. I've already talked with a developer. He's interested in a hundred acres of view property."

"You told me yesterday you need every bit of land you've got in order to make the ranch profitable. What happened overnight to change your mind?"

"Your father happened, all right? He's calling in the loan. If I don't sell off something—"

"You don't have to sell *anything*. The loan is covered."

"Why are you doing this? Why?"

"Because I'm your wife, damn it!" She jabbed him in the chest with her finger. "And because I love you."

She gasped. She hadn't meant to blurt out the truth. It had been an idiotic thing to say. He wasn't ready to hear how she felt. Not even close. And now he was gaping at her as if she'd grown a second head—or had lost her mind. Which was probably true.

She turned back to the stove. "Dinner's ready."

REED DIDN'T MAKE love to her that night.

Nothing could have hurt her more.

He didn't acknowledge her confession of love and certainly didn't profess any undying pledge to her. Over the next few days he withdrew into himself. They slept together but he didn't hold her.

He didn't love her.

Her body, her sensuality, reawakened after so many years of abstinence, cried out for his touch, his kisses. Her heart longed for what he had denied her—had denied them both.

It nearly drove Ann crazy. But it was what she'd agreed to—a marriage of *his* convenience. Though she might want to, she couldn't change the rules now. And apparently she wasn't as *convenient* as she had been before.

They'd been married one week to the day when the call came from the adoptions people. A social worker would visit that afternoon.

"I'll hire a substitute for my afternoon classes," Ann told Reed as she scurried around to get herself ready and Bets fed before her mother's arrival.

"You don't have to do that."

"Of course I do. The social worker will expect me to be here."

He didn't seem happy about the idea.

"Reed, this is why you married me. We're supposed to be a loving, *married* couple who want to adopt a baby."

He didn't acknowledge her comment. "You've got the letters of reference they wanted?"

"In the file folder on the coffee table. A school principal, the local bank manager and Dora, a successful businesswoman, whom I've known for years and who thinks we'll both make wonderful parents. That ought to cover it."

Grimly, he picked up his Stetson and placed it squarely on his head. "I'll see you this afternoon, then."

THE KINDEST DESCRIPTION of Clarisa Fipp would be plump. Making it from her car to the porch with a clipboard in hand had her breathing hard, and a sheen of perspiration dampened the social worker's forehead as introductions were made.

"What a lovely view," she said, pausing at the door to catch her breath.

"Every room in the house has a view," Ann commented. "And of course, there'll be plenty of room for Betina to play as she's growing up."

"Farms can be dangerous places for youngsters. All that heavy equipment and such."

Ann decided that in spite of the woman's pleasant smile, she was a born pessimist. "Come in, please. We're still getting settled and acquiring furniture but you'll see that the house is sound."

Reed held the screen door open for the Clarisa. "Bets has got her own room and crib and everything." He looked desperately uncomfortable, as though he were appealing his own death sentence before the supreme court instead of applying to adopt a baby. But for him, Ann suspected the stakes were just as high.

Ann gave him an encouraging smile, though the gamble she'd taken by marrying Reed and joining him in this scheme, carried a great deal of risk for her, too. Her stomach had been unsettled all day.

Clarisa gave the living room a cursory glance and then stuck her head into the kitchen. Fortunately Ann's mother had left it spotless before she left at noon. Amazingly, Reed and Eleanor Forrester had reached an uneasy accommodation with each other that at least allowed him some freedom to get his chores accomplished.

"Adequate," the social worker decided, making a note on her clipboard. "I am surprised to find a *Mrs.* Drummond, however. There's no notice of that on my form."

"We just got married last week," Reed stated. "I sent in the amendment to my application."

"Well, then, it will turn up. You know how slow we bureaucrats can be." She seemed not in the least contrite about the reputation of government workers. "Now let's have a look at our little bundle of joy, shall we?"

"She's *my* baby," Reed muttered under his breath. "Not *hers.*"

Ann silently shushed him. Now was not the time to talk back to a person in authority.

In a gesture of grandmotherly pride, Ann's mother

had decorated Betina's room in a Little Bo-Peep decor, with a padded crib bumper, matching sheets and a cover plate for the light switch. A new mobile dangled above the bed—musical lambs.

"Oh, my, she does look healthy, doesn't she," Clarisa cooed. Reed visibly tensed as she stroked Betina's soft cheek without waking the child.

As they returned to the living room, Ann talked with the social worker about Betina's feeding and sleeping schedule, though Reed would have been better qualified to answer her questions. Fortunately she was able to respond intelligently and with far more patience than she imagined Reed could muster.

"I'll be writing up my report when I get back to the office," Clarisa concluded. "On the surface, I see no impediments to—"

Someone knocked on the door.

"I'll get it," Reed said.

Ann wondered who it could be. They didn't get social callers, and Jason had been told not to come to work today. "You were saying, Ms. Fipp..."

Reed shoved open the screen to admit Johnny Fuentes, who was dressed in a dark blue police chief's uniform. His expression was anything but pleased, however.

Ann got a seriously uncomfortable feeling. Though she'd known Johnny since high school, he wouldn't be here unless there was a problem. Visions of her parents being in a car accident flooded her imagination.

"What is it, Johnny?" she asked a little desperately.

He glanced around the room. "I went by school thinking I'd catch you there after classes were over."

"I left early. Reed and I had an appointment with Ms. Fipp from the adoption department."

"Mr. Dunlap said you'd probably be here."

Reed said, "This isn't a real good time, Fuentes. If there's something wrong—"

"I'm more sorry about this than I can say, but I'm here to arrest you, Ann." Keeping one eye on Reed, he produced a pair of handcuffs from his back pocket. "You have the right to remain silent—"

Chapter Nine

Reed grabbed Johnny by the arm. "What the hell do you think you're doing?" Every protective instinct he had was screaming. This was his *wife* Fuentes was talking about.

"Don't interfere, Drummond," John warned. His eyes had narrowed, his lips thinned. "This is official business."

"You can't mean you're arresting *me*," Ann protested. She'd turned a chalky white and her eyes were wide in alarm.

The social worker clasped her clipboard to her chest like a shield. "Oh, my...oh, my..."

"Turn around, Ann," the police chief ordered.

"What in heaven's name are you arresting me *for*?"

"A storekeeper in San Luis Obispo where you've been passing bad checks identified you from your newspaper picture—"

"The Teacher-of-the-Year Award?"

"There's some mistake, buddy. You know Ann wouldn't—"

"My God, Johnny," Ann pleaded. "We went to school together—"

"I hate this more than I can tell you, Ann." A handcuff snicked closed around Ann's wrist. "The storekeeper says you're into him for a hundred dollars' worth of bad checks."

"That's utter nonsense. Why would I—"

"Don't cuff her, man. She's not resisting."

The social worker sputtered, "I really think I should go."

Reed shot her a quelling look. "Stay put a minute. We'll get this straightened out."

Ann looked at Reed frantically. "I haven't done anything—"

"I know," he said grimly. "Come on, John. Give us a break. You've known Ann longer than I have. You must realize—"

"There are fingerprints, Drummond. They're a little smeared but it looks like they'll be a match."

"*Looks* like? You can't put me in jail because my prints *look* like somebody's who wrote a bad check. They have to be identical."

"At this point, the similarities are pretty convincing. They're faxing them over from San Luis Obispo."

"Not good enough, buddy," Reed said. "Close only counts in—"

"The charge will stick if the shopkeeper IDs her." Without cuffing Ann with the second bracelet, he took her by the arm. "I'm going to put her in a lineup."

"A lineup?" Ann gasped.

Reed blocked John's path to the front door. "How'd you even get Ann's fingerprints to check? She's not exactly a convicted felon, for God's sake."

"Her prints are on record because she's a schoolteacher. Now, step aside."

His hands balling into fists, Reed didn't budge. "You're wrong, damn it!"

"It's all right, Reed," Ann said shakily. "Once I'm at the police station, I'm sure everything will get cleared up."

"I'm coming with you."

"You can't. You have to take care of Bets. This won't take long, I'm sure."

Reed wasn't so sure. He'd had a few run-ins with the law. To a man, the police were hardheaded and didn't listen well. If Fuentes thought he had Ann dead to rights on some fraudulent check-cashing deal, he'd be hard to convince otherwise.

Helplessly, he watched as the cop put Ann in the back seat of his black-and-white. This was crazy! Ann was so damn pure, she probably didn't even jaywalk.

"You do know, Mr. Drummond, that this incident…" The social worker fumbled for words and fanned herself with her clipboard. "If your wife has a criminal record that would certainly affect your petition to—"

"She's innocent!"

"Yes, well…we'll just have to wait and see, won't we? But I will have to include this new information in my report.'' With an awkward gait, she descended the steps to her car.

"You'd better be sure there's something in your report about innocent until proven guilty.''

Reed cursed long and low. This screwy mix-up had come at the worst possible time. How could Fuentes be fool enough to arrest Ann for something she couldn't possibly have done? Damn it all! She didn't have a criminal bone in her body. Ann had no reason to pass bad checks. Hell, she had more money than Reed did.

But the impact on Bets's adoption could be disastrous. Now not only would Reed have to get his wife out of jail, he'd have to convince a damn social worker it had all been a mistake in the first place.

HUMILIATION FILLED Ann with icy cold.

She shivered in the stark cell they'd assigned her. She'd been made to place her watch, earrings and gold wedding band in a brown envelope, which the booking officer had carefully sealed with tape, laboriously writing her name on the flap. Then he'd taken her fingerprints. Ann had nearly gagged on the chemical smell.

The camera flash when they'd taken her photo had blinded her; the indignity of the entire process mortified her.

Finally a female officer had taken her shoes, giving her thin stretch slippers as a replacement. Ann thought the woman had had children in her math classes, but she couldn't be sure. At this point, she couldn't think clearly about anything.

She had no idea how long she'd been here. Or why someone hadn't come to release her. There'd been no lineup. As far as she could tell, the entire world had forgotten about her.

Where was Reed? Was he trying to bail her out? Where on earth would he get the money?

She was so cold her teeth chattered. The stainless steel bunk she sat on was hard and comfortless; the pale green bars of her cell mocked her need for privacy.

Oh, God, where was Reed?

The heavy door that separated the holding cells from the squad room swung open.

"Sorry you've had to wait so long," Johnny said. He had her shoes in his hand.

She came to her feet, her knees weak with relief. "Does that mean I can go now?"

"Not yet. The victim had trouble finding someone to watch his shop so he could get away from the store. He's here now for the lineup."

"He'll tell you I'm not the one."

Without comment, Johnny handed her her shoes. A thousand times when they'd been in school together, she'd seen the quick flash of his smile when he was flirting with other girls. Now he was grim.

After she put on her shoes, he escorted her out of the holding area and into a small room with a big mirror on one wall. Three other women filed in with her, all of them with blond hair, though that's where their resemblance ended. Ann had watched enough cop shows on TV to know that her accuser was watching on the opposite side of the mirror.

Nervously, she shoved her hair back behind her shoulder.

"That's her, that's the one," an unseen man shouted. "She done that all the time, that hair thing with her hand."

A door slammed shut, and then the voices were muffled.

The other women looked at her suspiciously.

"I didn't do it," she whispered in a choked voice. Her chin trembled. Her whole world had turned topsy-turvy. How could some total stranger identify her as having written bad checks? She'd never done that in her life; she'd never once overdrawn her account. For God's sake, she was a math teacher! Even if she'd made an error in addition or subtraction, it wouldn't have been intentional.

Johnny took her back to the holding cell. She sensed in other circumstances he'd let one of his officers handle someone who'd been identified as a criminal. She supposed she ought to be grateful for the special treatment.

She wasn't.

"You know this is a terrible mistake, don't you?"

"I only wish it were." He opened the cell for her. "It was a positive ID, Ann. Along with your fingerprints, smeared or not, it looks bad for you. Even the handwriting on the check looks like yours."

"It's not." In spite of her overwhelming fear and humiliation, she squared her shoulders. "As soon as I get out of here, I'll prove it."

"I hope so, Ann. I really do." But he didn't look convinced it would be possible.

"I keep thinking this can't be happening to me."

"Drummond's got an attorney for you. He'll have you out on OR in a bit."

"OR?"

"Own recognizance. I didn't think you'd be a flight risk."

A flight risk? Where on earth would she go? This was her home. She'd grown up here. People *knew* her. She had a reputation to maintain. Since her one slip as an adolescent, she'd been circumspect about everything she did. Everything!

Until she'd married Reed. And then her heart had overruled her caution.

Barely averting the hysteria that threatened, she nodded numbly at Johnny. At least she was grateful that Reed hadn't had to put up bail, and then wondered how he'd managed to hire an attorney. Most of them demanded a deposit.

She waited for what seemed like another eternity before the door opened and she was finally released. Reed introduced her to an attorney named Marvin Hutch, whose tailored suit and carefully styled gray hair made him look like a million bucks. She didn't recognize him from town. She was so weak with fatigue and grateful to have been released, she didn't care where he had come from. He said something about talking with her later, but his words barely registered. She simply wanted to put this awful place behind her.

Cupping her elbow, Reed ushered her to his truck, which was parked across the street from the police station. It was dark now, and the streetlights glowed eerily in a misting fog.

"Are you okay?" he asked, opening the door.

"Where's Bets?"

"I called your mom. She came up to the ranch."

Gratitude that her mother had responded when needed mingled with the misery filling Ann's chest. "Take me home, Reed. Please."

She sat rigidly on the passenger side as he pulled the truck out of the parking space. Her hands shook as she slipped her wedding ring back on her finger and tried unsuccessfully to put on her earrings. She didn't want to let go of what small amount of control she'd maintained all afternoon. If she lost it she might never get it back again.

Arrested. Booked. Charged with writing bad checks.

"I didn't recognize that attorney," she said, her chaotic thoughts hopping wildly from one impossibility to another.

"He's from San Luis Obispo."

"He looks expensive."

"He is. Fuentes said you'd need a good one."

Her head whipped around and she stared at Reed. His hat was drawn low on his forehead, his jaw set at a grim angle. "Where did you get the money?"

"I sold a few head of beef. That's why it took me a while to get the attorney over here."

"Oh, Reed, you shouldn't have. You're trying to build your herd. If you'd asked, I'm sure my father would have—"

"You're my responsibility, not his." Reed kept his eyes on the road.

Ann's desperate effort to control her emotions shattered. Tears welled and spilled down her cheeks. Reed had sacrificed a part of his herd to get her out of jail. In return, she'd very likely put his plan to adopt Bets at risk.

A sob caught in her chest, and her tears began to cascade. "I'm so sorry..."

To her surprise, he hooked his arm around her shoulders and pulled her across the seat so she could rest her head on his shoulder. The tender gesture brought another sob from her throat. Dear heaven! He was such a good man.

"You've got nothin' to be sorry for, sweet sugar-Annie. It's all some stupid mistake. You'll see. We'll get the mess straightened out. I promise."

She cherished his words and the warmth of his body, the feel of his muscular arm holding her, though she didn't necessarily believe his promise.

Something had gone strangely, frighteningly wrong with her life. She might never be the same again.

ELEANOR FORRESTER opened the ranch-house front door the moment the truck came to a stop out front.

"I've been worried sick, dear," she said, hugging Ann as she reached the porch. "Are you all right?"

Ann nodded, though she'd never felt less right in her life.

"She'll be fine," Reed said grimly, his hand possessively palming the small of her back. "Is Bets asleep?"

"She went down like the little lamb she is," Eleanor announced.

"Thanks for coming."

It was a dismissal, and Eleanor took it as such, gathering up her purse before giving Ann another quick kiss on the cheek. "A good night's sleep, and you'll be right as rain, dear."

Ann was too numb to comment. Dazed, she stood in the middle of the living room staring at the miniature Dream Man on the mantel piece, her rogue cowboy and the baby he loved so much.

"What did the adoption worker say about my arrest?"

Reed stepped in front of her. "She's going to include it in her report."

"I'm so sorry," she repeated. Swallowing hard, she looked into his troubled eyes, seeing only a hint of the bad boy he'd once been. "Everyone's treating me like I'm a criminal."

"You're the most innocent woman I know."

"Then why do I feel so dirty?"

"An occupational hazard that comes from hanging around jails." Gently, he framed her face between his big hands. "I think I can fix it."

He lowered his mouth to hers in the sweetest kiss she'd ever known. He'd had coffee earlier, and the smooth, subtle invasion of his tongue brought with it the taste of sugar. The heat of him warmed the cold knot of humiliation that had lodged in her midsection. Her tension eased, and she responded with a soft moan of pleasure. Dear Lord, how much she'd missed him.

With artful skill, he slid her blouse from her shoulders. His fingers slipped beneath her bra straps and his knuckles skimmed the swell of her breast. She drew in a quick breath as her nipples puckered.

"Reed…"

"A shower is the perfect cure for what ails you."

A shower wasn't precisely what was on her mind. But she didn't object as he led her into the bathroom. He reached into the stall shower to turn on the water.

"You don't have to do this," she objected. "I can manage."

"I want to."

All she seemed able to do was stand patiently while he removed the rest of her clothes. To keep her balance, she rested her hand on his shoulder as he bent to remove her slacks one leg at a time. He'd had his hair trimmed in anticipation of the social worker's visit, and it lay smoothly at his nape. Where had his gentleness come from? In spite of the way he'd been raised, she'd seen it with Betina. And now with her.

Steam billowed, mixing in the air with his uniquely masculine scent.

"In you go," he ordered.

"Thank you." But he wasn't done with her yet.

He stripped off his shirt and sat down on the stool to remove his old worn boots.

Her eyes widened. "What are you doing?"

His raffish grin said it all.

"Reed, I don't think—"

"Exactly. You let me do the thinking for now."

Lathering his hands, he bathed her from head to toe. She was open and vulnerable, unable to escape him in the narrow confines of the shower stall. Not that she wanted to. His calloused hands caressed her with incredible tenderness, awakening thousands of nerve endings on her sensitive flesh in ways she hadn't known possible. His ministrations were so caring, so thorough, she felt as though he were worshiping her.

She'd never known such intimacy. Tears formed, and she let them slide down her cheeks. He kissed them away.

When the water began to cool, he wrapped her in thick towels and carried her to their bed, where he made exquisite love to her.

"You are so perfect," he whispered, his kisses raining down on her flushed skin. "I don't deserve you."

"That's not so."

Once again he ignored her objection, sweeping her up in a sensual assault that she had no intention of resisting.

For the first time she felt he wasn't simply using her. He was giving something of himself. Where her other efforts had failed, her arrest had touched him in some inexplicable way. Perhaps it was only that he now felt she needed him. But whatever the reason, there was a crack in his armor that hadn't been there before.

She relished it. Returning every bit of passion he

gave her, Ann sought to widen the path that led to Reed's heart. If she could do that, she might yet bless the confusion that had made her an accused criminal.

Lifting her hips, he drove into her one final time, and she lost track of all rational thought. The pleasure of her climax burst through her. She called his name, and he shouted hers in reply, throwing his head back as he gave himself over to the experience of total release. "Ann!"

For the first time he'd spoken her name intimately, without a "sugar" coating. At some intuitive level, she suspected that small omission was more meaningful than he was likely to admit anytime soon.

They lay together for a long while, their breathing slowing, their bodies damp.

Reed rolled to his side, bringing her with him, her head resting on his chest. She snuggled closer. Beneath her palm she felt the solid beat of his heart.

"You know, I'm really not perfect," she said when she'd recovered her breath. If she'd once had doubts about her love for him and the wisdom of her runaway emotions, she had none now. In the way he'd given of himself tonight, her confidence level had gone off the scale—half again more than a ten.

He grunted noncommittally.

"Don't put me on a pedestal, Reed. I've made as many mistakes as the next person." She needed to let him know she had human frailties, too. That once she'd been bad and had paid a desperate price.

"You look good on a pedestal. You've had a hard day. Get some sleep."

"Not before you hear the truth about me." She told him how she'd gone off with the town bad boy when she'd been seventeen. They'd lived high on the hog for a few weeks, until Jerry's money had run out and she'd become a nag about him getting a job. When he'd simply left her in that dingy San Diego motel, she'd had no choice but to call her parents to come get her.

As she told Reed about the baby she'd lost, tears crept from her eyes to land on his chest, but on the inside the ache seemed to ease. No one except her parents had ever heard this story. Until now.

Until Reed.

She lay there waiting for his reaction. "You still awake?" she asked.

He cleared his throat as though he'd been moved by her story. "Yeah, I'm awake." Gently he slid his fingers through her hair. "You were a kid, Ann. You can't keep beating yourself up for what happened so long ago."

"I should have known better."

Levering himself up on one elbow, he caressed her cheek with his fingertips. "That idiot hurt you, sweetheart. If I could get my hands on him right now I'd make him pay. But I can't do that, not after so much time. And you're so damn softhearted, you probably wouldn't let me anyway."

"Probably not," she whispered. His gentleness, his compassion made more tears well in her eyes.

"And I understand better now why Bets is so important to you. God, I'm sorry about your baby. You didn't deserve that.''

"I always felt…" Her voice caught. "I'd been so stupid."

"We've all done stupid things, me included. More than I'd care to admit. But what you did wasn't the end of the world. You survived. And you're the strongest, most courageous, most loving woman I know.''

His praise was a balm to her conscience, and she basked in his words like the sun had come out after years of darkness.

"I care about you, sweet sugar. More than you'll ever know, I care."

He showed her just how much by loving her again. And in telling Reed of her past, Ann knew she had cleansed herself more thoroughly than soap and water had managed in the past thirteen years. She loved Reed even more for not believing her one lapse in behavior had doomed her to a life beyond redemption.

Slowly, she felt the pain of the past—while not forgotten—ease away as he loved her. For that, she would always be grateful to Reed no matter what happened between them.

Just before she drifted off to sleep, she whispered, "I love you, Reed." Given the steady rhythm of his breathing, she doubted her heard her.

REED WAS DEAD ASLEEP when Bets woke him with her hungry cries at 3 a.m.

"I'll get her," Ann mumbled, though Reed doubted she was actually awake. "My...baby."

"Sleep, sugar. My turn."

As he eased himself out of bed, untangling his legs from Ann's, she moaned softly, rolling to the spot he had just vacated almost as if she didn't want him to leave. He stood a moment at the bedside looking at her in the pale light. Her hair spilled like moonbeams across the pillow; her slightly open mouth invited a kiss, as did the bare arm she'd stretched out in search of him. He'd like nothing better than to wake her with kisses.

But duty called, he reminded himself as he responded to Bets's increasingly insistent cries.

He hadn't intended to become responsible for Ann, any more than he had for Betsy and her boyfriend Tommy. Reed wasn't the kind of man people relied on. Until a few months ago, he'd been a rolling stone. He couldn't help but think his new image of daddy and husband was all a sham. Somebody would catch on that he was a fraud.

Then he'd lose it all.

He'd be back to being a loner with a mutt for a partner and a tired old horse who had barely escaped a trip to the glue factory. The prospect was not a happy one.

But the way his life had gone, he'd better brace himself for that eventuality. It wasn't smart to care too much. It didn't matter that Ann had twice blurted out that she loved him. He didn't dare believe that. If he did, it would hurt too much when she left him.

He lifted Bets to his shoulder and went in search

of her bottle. She nuzzled against his throat. His muscles worked, but he had trouble swallowing the lump that had formed.

He probably shouldn't have made love to Ann the second time tonight. But doing without her, not making love to her, had been the hardest thing he'd ever done in his life. Tonight he'd weakened because she'd needed him. Now she'd damn well be a hard habit to break. Just about as hard as if the adoption people decided he'd never have a chance to hold Bets again.

YOUNGSTERS WERE scurrying down the hallway and the first bell had already sounded by the time Ann got to her classroom the next morning. To her surprise, the door stood open.

"Ms. Forrester. Ms. Forrester," the principal called, hurrying in her direction.

"Mrs. Drummond," she quietly corrected as she noted a woman standing behind her desk sorting through lesson plans.

"I'm glad I caught you before you got to class." Breathing hard, Mr. Dunlap came to a halt beside Ann.

"The second bell's about to ring. I'm a little late and I need to—"

"I'm truly sorry, Ms. For—, ah, Mrs. Drummond, but I've taken the liberty of employing a substitute for your classes today."

She gaped at him. "What on earth for?" Not that she couldn't use a day off after the stress of her arrest yesterday but the children depended on her to be there. No matter how difficult her personal problems, she had no intention of failing her students.

"I thought, under the circumstances, you'd understand—"

"What circumstances?"

"Your arrest, of course." His cheeks colored with a blush. "The whole town's atwitter about it."

"I can imagine," she said with a grimace. "But what does that have to do with hiring a substitute?"

"Well, really, Ms. For—Mrs. Drummond, we can't expose our children to criminals, now can we?"

"What are you talking about? I'm not a criminal, and you know it. In addition to the fact that people are supposed to be innocent until proven—"

"The superintendent called first thing this morning. The school board is distressed, as you can well imagine." He ran his fingers around a shirt collar that was obviously too tight.

"I'm distressed, too, Mr. Dunlap." And getting angrier by the minute. "But I haven't done anything wrong."

"Nonetheless, in order to protect the children from any undue influence, we feel it's in their best interests that a long-term substitute be employed."

"What are you saying? Last week I was Teacher of the Year, for God's sake. Nothing has happened that changes my ability to teach!"

"Please lower your voice, Ms. Forrester," he said in hushed tones, glancing at late arriving students.

"I'm Mrs. Drummond! And I'll talk as loud as I

want. You can't fire me. It's unconscionable and probably against the law. I'll go right to the union."

"Dear me." He fumbled nervously, adjusting his tie, and the color on his cheeks deepened to scarlet. "The superintendent had hoped you'd understand that as soon as this unfortunate matter is, ah, resolved, we would reinstate you. At full benefits and salary, of course. But meanwhile, the parents, you see...and the board." He shrugged helplessly.

Ann fumed, but it wasn't going to do her any good. The decision had already been made by the powers on high. She could sue, of course. But by the time anything was settled, school would be out for the summer.

Meanwhile, her good name—her reputation— would be totally ruined. Which was the only reason Reed had married her.

All she could do was discover as quickly as possible who was falsely accusing her, and why, and who the real culprit was.

Her career, her marriage and her chance to be Betina's mother were all hanging in the balance. Not to mention her ability to make payments on the second mortgage she'd just taken out on her house.

THAT NIGHT, after Reed made love to her, Ann had trouble falling asleep. It wasn't that he hadn't done a superb job of satisfying her physically. He had, for which she was ever so grateful. But she was too on edge to relax. Her mind reeled at all that had happened to her in the past few weeks.

She slipped out of bed without waking Reed and

went to Betina's room. The lamb mobile moved slightly above the crib as she pulled up a chair. When she stroked the baby's hand, feeling the softness of her skin, Betina's fingers curled around hers, holding on tight.

"I love you," Ann whispered, leaning her head against the crib slats. "I love your daddy, too. He doesn't believe that yet, but I'm trying, my little lamb. I want us to be a family. I'm going to fight for us, baby." She set her heart firmly, stubbornly, against any other outcome. "A real family."

Chapter Ten

Marvin Hutch's law offices were as plush as Ann
had anticipated, with thick carpeting, original oil
paintings on the walls and a view of the surrounding
hills from the third-floor windows. She shuddered to
think how many head of cattle Reed had had to sell
in order to pay for a few hours of the attorney's
time.

She'd been home for two days, waiting for her
appointment with the attorney, and was impatient for
a resolution to her problem. But having a chance to
be a full-time mom to Betina had been a reward of
sorts for the stress she'd been experiencing. She'd
played with the baby every minute she'd been
awake, fascinated by each coo and gurgle, and not
getting a thing done around the house. Even during
Betina's naps, Ann had watched her sleep. With
each passing moment, she'd dreamed and hoped for
the future.

She pictured being with Bets when she took her
first steps and seeing her eyes light up on Christmas

morning after Santa had arrived, taking her to school
on the first day of kindergarten.

The attorney cleared his throat. Reality intruded,
and Ann had to set those fanciful images aside.

Marvin tented his fingers beneath his chin. He sat
behind his large mahogany desk, the surface bare
except for a discreet photo of his family, a thin file
folder, a yellow notepad and a pen. Ann and Reed
sat in matching leather chairs opposite him.

"The total amount of money involved is not
large," Marvin said. "There are two checks in question for a total of less than fifty dollars. When the
penalty of twenty-five dollars per bad check is included, only a hundred dollars is in question. My
recommendation is that you pay Mr. Ulrich his
money."

"But that would be an admission of guilt," Ann
protested.

"Generally, if restitution is made, the charges are
dropped."

"I don't want them *dropped* that way. I'm innocent."

Reed covered her hand. "Easy, sugar. We need
to listen to the man."

"Yes, Mrs. Drummond, I understand that is your
position—"

"It's the truth. I never wrote those checks. You
can look at my check register, if you'd like."

"The presence of your fingerprint is a bit troubling, however."

"Troubling? It's insane. Besides, Johnny wasn't
even sure it was a match yet. It was smeared, for

God's sake." Reed might be trying to calm her, but Ann was in no mood for calm at all. Every time she thought about being locked up in that miserable cell, she got furious all over again.

Reed asked, "How did the guy get fingerprints at all? You'd think after a check has been handled through the whole bank deposit business, you'd never be able to identify anybody's prints."

"Apparently Mr. Ulrich experiences a fair number of bad checks at his convenience store. He has taken to having the customer place his or her thumbprint on the back of the check with a special ink."

"If I had been the one to write the checks, he could have let me know they'd bounced. I certainly would have made them good. But I *didn't* write them."

Marvin flipped open the file folder and withdrew two sheets of paper. "These are photocopies of the checks. In both cases, the signature is of a person named Jodie Sutherland. Have you ever been known by that name, Mrs. Drummond?"

"Of course not. I've never even heard of such a person." She studied the checks. As the police chief had mentioned, the handwriting was amazingly similar to hers. But it *wasn't* hers, damn it! "When is all of this supposed to have happened? If it was during school hours, I have a perfect alibi. Even Fuentes would have to believe I couldn't be in two places at once."

"I believe Mr. Ulrich mentioned something about early evening, though I would have to confirm that. Would you also have an alibi for that time of day?"

"It depends on what day, for heaven's sake. I live alone. Sometimes I work late at school." Her chin quivered with anger and frustration. Why wouldn't *anyone* believe her—except Reed? "There's an address here for the woman who wrote the check. Has anyone tried to find—"

"As I understand it from the San Luis Obispo police, a woman by that name did live at that address with her son for a short period. She no longer resides there and left no forwarding address."

"Well, I certainly don't have a son, so that woman can't be me."

Reed stretched out his legs, crossing his ankles. Though he'd put on his newer jeans that morning, his boots were anything but fancy. "Sounds like a case of mistaken identity to me."

"Maybe the problem is that I have a look-alike," Ann said thoughtfully. "Marcy McCullough—she has the classroom next to mine—said something about seeing me here in town one Saturday when I'd been at home." Ann didn't mention that had been day when Reed had proposed their unusual marital arrangement. "Come to think of it, Dora said something of the same thing once—seeing me here when I'd been in del Oro the whole day."

"Were it not for the thumbprint, I'd quite agree that the merchant has simply identified someone who resembles you," the attorney said.

"Well, then, the print is the problem. It's got to be a mistake or a fraud," Ann insisted.

"Or your identical twin is the culprit," Marvin suggested mildly. "Twins can have very similar though not identical prints. Actually, some siblings do as well.''

She almost laughed at that, but the whole situation was so serious she couldn't find much humor in it. "Not likely, Mr. Hutch. I'm an only child."

"Yes, well, it would have made for an interesting defense, at any rate. There have been some precedents set—" Frowning a little, he tapped his finger to his lips. "Were you, by chance, adopted, Mrs. Drummond?"

"I think you're barking up the wrong tree, Mr. Hutch."

"Are you sure your folks would have told you if you'd been adopted?" Reed asked.

"People don't keep that a secret these days," she said. "It's nonsense to think—"

"Adoptions were handled a little differently thirty years ago than they are today," Marvin stated. "Far more of the placements are handled by private attorneys than formerly, and most adoptions are open, with the birth mother actually choosing who will adopt her baby."

Frustration forced Ann to her feet. "We're not getting anywhere with this conversation. The problem is a mix-up in the fingerprints. Maybe the ones I have on file have been switched with someone else's. I don't know. But it seems unlikely I have some identical twin floating around that I've never heard of."

Marvin stood, too, as did Reed.

"I'll pursue other avenues, of course," Marvin said. "But indulge an old man's whims, if you would. Ask your parents if there is any possibility of a twin. Or even a mix-up at birth. Such a scenario would certainly explain our little mystery, wouldn't it?"

Reed placed his hat on his head and took Ann's hand. "We'll ask her mother," he said.

Ann thought it would be a waste of time but she couldn't very well argue. The sooner Mr. Hutch was convinced she was an only child born to Eleanor and Richard Forrester the sooner he'd get on with exploring the real reason she'd been charged with passing bad checks.

IT WAS LUNCHTIME when they left the attorney's office. Instead of heading home they stopped at a sandwich shop on the town's main street. Reed found them a corner table and went to order at the counter.

The place was filled with college students from the nearby university, most of them carrying backpacks and all of them looking well scrubbed. In his Stetson and jeans, Reed didn't fit into the crowd but they all moved aside for him. In addition to being taller and broader than most of the students, there was an air of self-assurance about him, a self-confidence that said "Don't mess with me."

None of these youngsters was about to challenge him for a spot at the counter. Particularly when his lips were tugged into such a grim line and his jaw held so tautly.

Fretfully, Ann turned the gold band on her finger. He must be worried sick about keeping his ranch and Bets. So far, instead of helping him, Ann had done nothing but bring him trouble. She'd never meant for that to happen. What she'd wanted was to show Reed about love. Her love. And he'd never once commented on the words she had spoken in such haste. It was as if he hadn't heard them. Or worse, that he was determined to reject both her and the deep feelings that filled her every waking moment—when she wasn't going crazy over this arrest mix-up.

He returned to the table with a ham-and-cheese sandwich on rye for her and a pastrami on a roll for himself, plus fries and soft drinks. She pulled several napkins from the dispenser and gave him a couple.

"Maybe I ought to just cover the bad checks and make all of this go away," she said.

"People who haven't done anything wrong shouldn't have to pay." He took a big bite of his sandwich, then picked up a fry.

She wasn't very hungry but tried a nibble of her sandwich. "That's a noble sentiment but perhaps it's past time for being noble."

"Let's give Hutch a few more days to figure out what's going on."

"And run up an even bigger bill in attorney fees? Without me working, how are we ever going to pay him?"

"We'll manage."

A burst of laughter came from a nearby table, and Ann leaned forward. "I don't want you to sell any more cattle. Or your land."

His lips twitched ever so slightly. "Look who's

being bossy. You went and got a loan on your house when I said no.''

"That was different. You needed the money. A hundred dollars would cover—"

"We'll wait."

"And if your adoption petition is turned down because your wife has a criminal record?"

His eyes narrowed. "It won't be."

Ann suspected his confidence was misplaced but her heart warmed at the way he was being so supportive of her. Most men who had arranged a marriage of convenience of this sort would surely walk away now. An annulment would be easy at this early stage—so easy she couldn't bring herself to voice the thought.

Apparently he had a thought he wasn't afraid to voice. "This mess started when you married me and your father saw to it my loan was called. Do you think there's a possibility that your father—"

"No! My father wouldn't do anything that would send me to jail." In spite of her denial, she wondered just how angry her father still was. She hadn't seen him since she'd announced her marriage to Reed, and she'd been afraid to ask her mother too many questions. But he was a man who had never liked being crossed. "He wouldn't," she reiterated, but less vehemently this time.

Back at the ranch, Arnold rounded the corner of the house as soon as he heard the truck approaching. His whole back end wagged its welcome as he escorted them the last hundred feet home.

Ann's mother was playing with Bets on the front

porch. She had the baby in a new stroller and Bets was contentedly gazing at the fascinating world around her. The promise of an early summer was in the warmth of the air along with the lingering scent of spring wildflowers.

"Hello, children," Eleanor called, waving as they got out of the truck. "I hope everything went well with the attorney."

Ann shrugged. "Not exactly."

Taking the steps two at a time, Reed reached the porch and knelt in front of his daughter. "Hey, sweet pea, how's daddy's little cowgirl? Miss your old man?"

In response, the baby waved her arms and happily gurgled her recognition. A bubble of milk formed on her lips, then popped, startling Bets.

Reed laughed, a low, masculine sound filled with love and caring.

Ann met her mother's gaze, and she saw the depth of tenderness in her eyes that matched her own. How could a woman not love a man like Reed?

"Where'd the stroller come from?" he asked.

"Oh, I was visiting with Mavis Caldwell last evening. She and I are in the same bridge club, you know. Have been for years. She keeps this stroller around for when her grandchildren visit and said I could borrow it for Bets."

He eyed her suspiciously. "You're doing too much for Bets, Mrs. Forrester. I don't want you to spoil her."

"Pshaw, young man. What's a grandmother for? And it's only borrowed."

He didn't look entirely satisfied with the answer. "I'll get her the stuff she needs. It'll just take a little time," he said, his pride and need for independence showing. Or maybe it was a reminder to Ann that she and her mother had no part of his long-term plans for either himself or his child.

"I know that, dear." Eleanor fussed with fringe around the stroller's sunshade. Her usually pristine blouse was streaked with a line of baby spit-up, which seemed not to concern her at all. "Oh, a certified letter came a bit ago. The mail carrier had me sign for it. It's from the county."

Reed's head snapped up. "From adoptions?"

"Well, now, I don't really know. It was for Ann..."

"For me?"

"I put it on the kitchen table, dear."

Curious, Ann went inside. She tossed her purse on the table and picked up the envelope. The address read Ann Forrester Drummond, a.k.a. Jodie Sutherland.

"What on earth?" Until today she'd never heard of Jodie Sutherland, and with each passing moment she was less and less thrilled that their paths had ever crossed.

She ripped the envelope open. With increasing shock and dismay, she read the contents. Dear God! The world had gone totally crazy!

Letter in hand, she marched back out onto the porch. "Reed!"

"Yeah?"

"I'm being sued by the county welfare department for fraudulently accepting benefits for myself and my dependent son.''

Both Reed and her mother stared at Ann.

"I don't get it," he said.

"What son?" her mother asked.

"Apparently they have me confused with this Jodie Sutherland woman." Seething, she handed Reed the letter. "According to the welfare department, since I, Ann Forrester Drummond, am gainfully employed producing more than a poverty-level income, I'm not eligible for aid to dependent children, even though they think I have a nonexistent minor child, whom I've never heard of. My filing a claim under an assumed name is fraud and they're threatening to file charges if I don't reimburse the county four thousand dollars.''

She slammed her fist against the porch railing. "Damn that woman! If I ever get my hands on her, I swear, I'm going to kill her.''

"I don't understand, dear. What are you saying?"

Reed jammed the letter back in the envelope. "She's saying her life has turned into a mess unless she was adopted as a baby and has an identical twin floating around out there somewhere, with practically identical fingerprints.''

Eleanor Forrester gasped and went deathly pale.

"Mother?" Ann went to her.

"I'm all right." Eleanor waved her away.

"Mrs. Forrester, if you know something about this mess your daughter is in, you've got to tell her. She could go to jail if you don't.''

"Oh, my…" Her hand flew to her throat, and she

looked around frantically and her complexion went from pale to bright red.

"Sit down, Mother." Ann helped her to the wooden bench that was on the porch. "Reed, get her a glass of water. Please."

"She knows something."

"Go." Ann settled down next to her mother, holding her hand and soothing her, but on the inside Ann's emotions were churning. She couldn't imagine why her mother had reacted so strongly to the suggestion that she'd been adopted. Or that there might be a twin.

Reed returned with a glass of water.

Eleanor drank half of it and handed it to Ann. "You're my daughter, you know."

"Yes, Mom, I know."

"And Richard's, too. I know he can be demanding and overbearing sometimes, but he has always loved you so much. You know that, don't you, dear?"

"Of course I do." As a child, she'd been Daddy's little angel. Never once had she doubted or questioned her parents' love. And only once had she rebelled at the restrictions they'd imposed.

Her mother sobbed a tiny sound. "We kept putting off telling you..."

"Telling me what?"

"And then it seemed, well, too late."

"It's not too late now, Mother."

Eleanor reached up to stroke her daughter's cheek. "You were such a pretty baby and I loved you so much. I still do. I couldn't have loved you any more if you had come from my own body."

Ann's world, a world that had so recently begun to spin out of control, took another wild revolution. The mental gyration made Ann feel sick to her stomach. "Are you saying I'm adopted?"

Reed's hand gently closed over her shoulder in a touch that was meant to reassure. Ann was too stunned by her mother's revelation to respond to anything beyond the startling news that she might not be her parents' biological child.

Eleanor, tears in her eyes, nodded. "After a while, it didn't seem like we'd have to tell you. You were our little baby. Nobody else's. Can you understand that?"

Ann could barely accept she'd been lied to all of her life, much less understand it. It was as if she'd been standing on a trapdoor all these years and finally someone had released the latch. She was falling, she couldn't catch her breath, and she hadn't hit bottom yet.

"Mrs. Forrester, do you know if Ann was a twin?"

Eleanor blinked up at him. "Oh, dear, no. If she had been, we would have happily taken both babies. I'd always wanted a big family and so had Richard. We never would have separated her from a sister or brother."

Giving Ann's shoulder another reassuring squeeze, Reed thought the more likely possibility was a sister—an identical twin. Ann's current problems would make a kind of twisted sense if that was the case. He was a logical man and that would provide a logical explanation, *if* he could prove there was a twin. Better yet, if he could find her.

"Mrs. Forrester, did you adopt Ann through a state agency, or was it a private adoption?"

"We used an attorney in San Luis Obispo. The mother was a local girl, I'm sure. Though we didn't meet her, you understand. She was young, you see, and had gotten herself into trouble with a boy who ran with a wild crowd. From a good family, the attorney assured us."

"Yes, I'm sure." As Reed tried to learn the facts of Ann's adoption, he noted Ann had gone mute. She was barely breathing. He could only imagine the shock she'd experienced and wondered how she'd deal with the news.

What he needed to do now was get as much information as he could from Eleanor Forrester about Ann's adoption, and then figure out how to track down Jodie Sutherland, who had to be Ann's twin, assuming that was her real name. Meanwhile, he had to help Ann come to terms with the blow she'd received. He suspected the latter task might, in the long run, be the most difficult. Children could handle almost anything except their parents lying to them.

Grimly, he swore he would never lie to Bets—about anything.

"JASON'S HERE," Ann announced, her voice devoid of emotion. She was standing at the window gazing outside, her arms wrapped around herself. She'd barely spoken at all since her mother had left a half hour ago after putting Bets down for a nap. Reed didn't know what to say, how to help. Or even how to get through to her.

"I'll send him home," he said.

"No. He needs you."

"What about you?"

She gave a weary shake of her head. "I think right now I need to be alone."

He reached up to stroke her hair, to lift the golden-brown strands behind her shoulder, but then withdrew his hand. "We'll talk later, okay?"

She shrugged. "There isn't much to say."

Feeling helpless, he jammed his hands into his pockets. "Nothing's really changed, you know."

Looking up at him, she said, "Not changed? How can you say that? I don't even know who I am anymore."

"You're still the same person—"

"Please, Reed." There was a desperate plea in the depths of her emerald eyes, and a lot of pain. "Go do whatever you need to with Jason. I'll listen for Bets."

He didn't want to argue with her. He also didn't want to leave her when she looked on the verge of losing it. Indecisive, he glanced toward where the kid had dropped his bike and was looking for him in the barn.

"Go," she whispered, ordering him out. "I'll be fine."

Snatching up his hat from the coffee table, he

said, "I'll fix sandwiches for dinner. You just...take it easy, okay?"

She didn't acknowledge his suggestion as he went out the front door. The way she was acting, she probably didn't care if she ate at all. Reed guessed he could understand that. But it made him feel damn impotent that he couldn't do anything to help her.

"Come on, let's get some shingles up onto the roof," he said to Jason.

The boy tipped his head back to look at the roof and swallowed hard. "Five bucks an hour, right?"

"You have to earn it, not just talk about it."

With grudging enthusiasm, the kid helped Reed secure a bundle of shingles to a rope, which Reed hauled up to the roof. When they'd finished the second bundle, Reed said, "You want to muck out Fiero's stall or help me nail these suckers in place?"

"Some choice," the boy muttered.

But he followed Reed up the ladder, as Reed knew he would, and hunkered down beside him. It looked like he had some idea how to handle a hammer so Reed showed him how to lay the shingles by overlapping them.

"Is what they say about Ms. Forrester true?" Jason asked after a while.

"What are they saying?"

"That she's gonna go to jail."

"Nope. She hasn't done anything wrong."

The boy hit his thumb with the hammer and swore. "I told 'em they were full of it. I had to knock Buddy Jenkins in the teeth to get him to shut up."

Edging down the roof line, Reed swallowed a smile. The kid was probably half in love with Ann himself. "You're not supposed to fight. You'll get in trouble with Dunlap."

"It don't matter."

"Yeah, it does. I'll cut your wages."

"Hey, man! That's not fair."

"Then don't get yourself into a fight."

Jason didn't seem happy with the threat, but Reed suspected the kid would think twice before using his fists the next time. That seemed like a step in the right direction. He figured Ann knew what she was talking about. The kid needed the firm hand of a decent father to keep him on track. Too bad he didn't have one.

"You remember your ol' man?" Reed asked, duckwalking to lay down the next shingle.

"Naw. He took off before I was born. Mom said he was a real loser."

"So why'd she hook up with him?"

The kid shrugged. "She always did that, pick losers, I mean. There was always some guy around."

"It must have been hard, living like that."

"Some of 'em were okay."

From the words Jason left out, Reed suspected some of them beat the hell out of the kid. Not an unusual situation, he supposed. But Jason deserved better—deserved better than a temporary foster home, too. But Reed couldn't change that.

They worked their way along the roof, Reed doubling back so his line of shingles didn't get too far ahead of Jason's.

"So how come you married Ms. Forrester?"

Reed cut the boy a look. His questions were getting a little too personal. "Why do you think?"

The adolescent grin he got in return deserved to be wiped off with Reed's fist. But that wouldn't exactly set a good example for the boy, particularly after the lecture he'd just given him about not fighting.

And in truth, Reed was no longer entirely sure why he'd married Ann. He'd told himself it had been to ensure he'd get to adopt Betina. That Ann was the sexiest woman he'd ever known—and more than willing to sleep with him—was a bonus.

But with all of this business of her arrest, and now learning that she'd been adopted, he'd been feeling protective of her. Possessive. Entirely too much so.

Their arrangement was a temporary one. That's all she'd agreed to. He couldn't count on more than that. If he had any sense, he wouldn't even want to. That way he wasn't likely to care when she walked out the door.

Everyone else he'd cared about had done just that.

As HE'D EXPECTED, Ann barely touched her sandwich. Not that bologna was her favorite gourmet meal, he supposed. But she hadn't shown any interest in feeding Bets, either, or playing with her. The shock of her mother's revelations had turned Ann into a zombie, and Reed didn't know what to do.

By the time he cleaned up the kitchen and got Bets settled for the night, Ann had already gone to bed. He showered and got into bed beside her, pull-

ing her over to spoon against him. With a force of
will, he kept his libido in check. It wasn't easy.
Whenever he touched sweet sugar-Annie, he wanted
her. Those few nights when he'd denied himself the
pleasure of her body had been a purgatory he
wouldn't like to repeat. At the same time he knew
that not having her would be his eventual fate.

Tonight, though, he needed to make her talk.
Shocking her out of her lethargy seemed a reasonable way to start. Not that he'd read many books on
psychology. This time he'd simply have to wing it.

"So I guess you're going to sue your folks, huh?"

Chapter Eleven

Ann's eyes flew open. She'd been playing possum, not wanting to deal with Reed or even think about what an unbelievable day this had been.

"Why on earth would I want to do that?" she asked.

"Well, they lied to you, didn't they?"

"Not because they wanted to hurt me."

"You mean they love you?"

"Of course. I've never once doubted—" Twisting around, she glared at him. He'd left the light on in the bathroom and it sliced across the bed, leaving his features in dark silhouette. What little control she'd maintained all afternoon threatened to shatter when she realized what he was trying to do. "You don't have to try to make me feel better."

"I wouldn't think of it. Just commenting, is all."

The hell he was. He was trying to get her to look at things objectively. She couldn't do that. Not yet. The ache in her chest was too painful, the weight of what her parents had done too heavy. "I feel so betrayed," she cried. "Why didn't they tell me?"

"Because they love you." He echoed her earlier words, and in whatever context, she knew they were true. But that didn't seem to ease the ache.

"What would have been so awful if they'd told me the truth?"

"They were probably scared spitless they'd lose you."

"That's ridiculous. They're the only parents I've ever known."

"Easy for you to say," he mocked gently. "You've never adopted a kid. It can be pretty damn scary. What if Bets grows up and says she's sorry her mom gave her to me. You know how much that would hurt?"

"It's not going to happen, Reed. You're wonderful with—"

"Ask her if she feels that way the first time I have to ground her because she stayed out past curfew with some pimply faced kid who gave her a hickey."

Admittedly, that conjured up an image Ann would love to see—not that she would wish trouble on Reed and his daughter. She just wasn't sure she had much chance of sticking around that long.

"Adopting a kid is like walking a tightrope, sugar. I guess all parents make mistakes, but they can be real biggies if the kid is only on loan to you."

"How come you're suddenly such a big defender of my parents? Particularly my father?"

Reed pulled her closer, all but forcing her to rest her head on his shoulder. She didn't resist. In the midst of her turmoil, he seemed like a safe haven, an anchor in her turbulent sea of emotions. His strength of character—often disguised behind a rebellious swagger—was one of the reasons she loved him.

"I don't like to see you going off half-cocked."

"I'm not doing that," she protested. "I'm shocked, is all. Anyone would be."

"And thinking only about yourself."

She frowned. That cut a little too close to the bone.

"Has it occurred to you that somewhere out there, based on what we now know, you probably have an identical twin sister?"

"Who lives on welfare and passes bad checks in her spare time," Ann said with distaste. At least she had never stooped that low, even during those difficult days after she'd run off with her adolescent boyfriend.

"And who maybe wasn't adopted by a family who loved her enough to take her back when she made a mistake."

That brought Ann up short. She decided Reed had a merciless talent for making people face the truth about themselves and others, whether they wanted to or not. While she might not particularly appreciate his wisdom at the moment, she had to admit he'd made a good point. She did, apparently, have a sister. During her childhood she'd envied the girls with sisters. For most of them there'd been a special bond of closeness that went beyond friendship. As an only child, she'd never known that.

"Of course," Reed added, "your twin is probably a lot cuter than you are."

Her head reared up. "How can you say that? If we're identical, we'd look just the same."

"On second thought, you're probably feistier."

She jabbed him in the ribs, and laughing, he flinched. "Reed Drummond, I'm going to get you for that."

"I certainly hope so." He captured her face between his big hands, pulling her to him for a kiss that was deep and hot and made her feel needy for more.

"Nobody could be feistier than you, sweet sugar," he said as he rolled her onto her back and began the slow, sensual lovemaking that she hungered for.

It wasn't long before the revelations of the day drifted from Ann's mind. In Reed's arms, all she could think about was him—the feel of his hands caressing her intimately, the stroke of his tongue in private places, and the way her heart would always belong to her sweet, gentle rogue cowboy.

HER FATHER SHOWED UP at the ranch early the next day. Reed was in the barn checking Fiero, and Ann had just fed Bets her morning bottle.

Though Ann didn't quite know what she'd say to her father, she knew she couldn't put off this long-overdue conversation. There were several subjects that needed to be explored—and explained.

Lifting Bets to her shoulder and picking up a light blanket to protect her from the cool morning air,

Ann went outside to meet her father. He stopped at the foot of the porch steps.

"Hello, Daddy."

"Your mother says I'm in big trouble with you."

"I'm disappointed in you both. And hurt."

Dressed in khaki work pants and an old flannel shirt he liked to wear around the house, her father looked every bit of his seventy-some years. Somehow Ann hadn't noticed how quickly he was aging. Now her heart constricted at the thought of losing him. In spite of his bluster and domineering ways, he had been a solid influence in her life.

In an uncharacteristic show of remorse and uncertainty, he studied the tips of his old tennis shoes. "I'm sorry, angel. I wanted to be your father so badly, I thought if I never admitted you were adopted then there'd be no chance that I could lose you."

"Oh, Daddy..." Tears sprang to her eyes, and she went down the steps to hug him. His cheeks glistened damply by the time she reached him, and they held on to each other tightly.

He nearly squished both Ann and Bets in a desperate embrace. "Well, let's see this baby you've got."

Smiling at his gruffness, Ann lifted the blanket and turned so he could admire Bets.

"Tiny little thing, isn't she?" he commented with typical masculine understatement.

From the barn, Ann saw Reed marching with determined strides in her direction. She smiled slightly. He was quite a sight, a rugged cowboy hell-bent to rescue her—or his daughter. "Daddy, I want you and Reed to be friends."

He sputtered. "I don't know why you married that boy. If you ask me—"

"You don't get a vote." And at the moment, her vote and Reed's were tied about how long this marriage would last.

Her father gave her a belligerent look. "All I ever wanted was what's best for you."

"Fine. Then you'll see to it Reed's line of credit is extended again."

"Is that the price I have to pay to gain your forgiveness?"

"It's the *right* thing to do, and you know it, because you're the one who taught me everyone deserves a second chance. That ought to include my husband."

His face turned the shade of a vermilion sunset as Reed reached the house.

"What's happening?" His expression hard-edged, Reed looped his arm protectively around Ann's shoulders.

"My father was just explaining how the bank's loan officer made a mistake when he canceled your line of credit. As soon as he can get into town, Dad is going to make sure things are straightened out."

"I'm not looking for charity, Mr. Forrester. If the bank doesn't want to make the loan, I'll find another way to make a go of the ranch."

"Not necessary, young man." With grim determination, her father glanced around at the house and the barn. "Now that I see the place, it's in better shape than I remembered. I'm sure Roger Clarke will be willing to reconsider his earlier decision."

"And if I don't want the bank's money?"

Ann elbowed Reed in the ribs. *Lord save her from men who'd sooner have pride than porridge to fill their empty bellies.* "Reed will appreciate anything you can do, Daddy."

"Yes, well…" Looking ill at ease, her father slid his hands in his pants pockets. "Now that we got that settled, what are you planning to do about this arrest nonsense? I've tried talking to Fuentes but he won't listen."

Bets started to fuss, and Reed took the baby from Ann. "We're going to track down Ann's twin," he said.

"We are?" This was the first time he'd mentioned his plan to Ann, though it made sense. If she hadn't been so upset she would have thought of it herself. But how could they find her if the police had failed?

Her dad scowled. "That attorney your mother and I used never mentioned a twin."

"There's no other logical explanation for this mix-up, so that means she's out there somewhere," Reed insisted. "Finding her is the only way to clear Ann's name and get this mess straightened out with both the police and the adoption people."

Ann appreciated Reed's determination. She'd like it even more if his resolve hadn't been motivated by his need for a wife with a spotless reputation. Her chest tightened. Despite all of her efforts, she'd made little impact on his heart.

"I'll hire a private detective," Richard said. "It shouldn't be all that difficult to find the woman."

"And her son," Ann added.

Reed's expression was less defensive now as he studied her father than it had been earlier. "Why don't you let me give it a shot first? Keeping this whole thing unofficial may open some doors."

With obvious reluctance, Richard Forrester agreed to Reed's plan. He might not trust Reed but he was trying to give him a second chance. That small step forward pleased Ann.

After her father left, Reed said, "Since I'm going to get my line of credit back, that means you can cancel the second mortgage you took on your house."

"There's no rush. You can use what you need to upgrade your equipment or buy more—"

"I told you before, I need to do this on my own. That's why I had you sign the prenuptial. If you don't talk to the bank, I will."

"Fine!" In frustration, she spat out the word. "If you don't want my help, so be it. But I'm your *wife*, damn it! And as long as I am, we're in this business together. You help me clear my name and I help you with the ranch. You can use my money or not. I don't care. When we call it quits, and only then, I'll talk to the bank. You got it?"

He scowled at her but didn't offer any argument. Ann didn't fool herself. She guessed they'd only reached a temporary truce, one that would last until they'd resolved all the other issues that were preventing Reed from adopting Betina. And loving Ann.

THAT AFTERNOON they left Bets with Ann's mother again and drove into San Luis Obispo.

Ann shuddered as they parked in front of a row of apartments in the poorest section of town, the address given on Jodie Sutherland's bogus checks. The six buildings were two-story boxes housing six apartments each. The paint was peeling, the stucco chipped. An occasional cracked window added to the general atmosphere of despair. A broken tricycle, cardboard boxes and an old tire were scattered about what used to be a postage-stamp-sized piece of grass that had long since reverted to weeds and cracked soil. A permanent Vacancy sign was stuck in the ground.

She slid out of the truck and gazed up at a second-floor window where the drapes hung in tatters. "How could anyone live here?"

Reed joined her on the sidewalk. "Makes you count your blessings, huh? And you can bet a kid like Jason has lived in worse."

Either Ann's twin was very much down on her luck or she had problems Ann didn't even want to contemplate. If they managed to find her, Jodie Sutherland's difficulties would be compounded by the bad checks she'd passed. For an instant, Ann felt a surge of sympathy for the stranger to whom she was very likely linked by blood.

On the other hand, it wasn't fair that Ann should take the blame for something her sister had done, particularly when it had cost her the job she loved and might cause Reed to lose Bets.

"Let's see if we can nose around, ask some questions," Reed said.

"I thought the police already investigated—"

"Folks in a place like this don't much like to talk to cops. Or private detectives. We might be able to do better."

After they'd knocked at a dozen doors and managed to leave their names at only a couple of apartments, Ann blew out a sigh. "This isn't going to work."

"You give up too easy, sugar. Somebody around here knows where Jodie's gone. Sooner or later she'll get the word we're looking for her."

But would she care? Ann wondered.

Eventually they covered the entire apartment complex, talking to anyone who would answer the door. One or two people looked as if they recognized Ann—or rather, momentarily mistook her for her twin. But they were close-mouthed about what they knew.

By the time they got back to the ranch, Ann was exhausted from the strain and ready for a hot soak in the tub. Relieving her mother of baby-sitting duties and sending her home, Ann decided to take advantage of a few moments' quiet to relax while Bets was napping. That's when she saw an ominous brown envelope on the kitchen table, so official-looking it gave her the shivers.

"Reed, there's a letter for you. From the Department of Adoptions."

Reed came out of the bedroom. He'd been changing into his work clothes and something in Ann's tone alerted him to trouble. Giving her a fleeting glance, he took the envelope and ripped it open.

Report on Adoption Petition
Minor child: Betina Shoemaker
Applicant Family: Reed and Ann Drummond
Caseworker: Clarisa Fipp, MSW

Reed scanned the bureaucratic gobbledygook, his stomach knotting on pap like "psychological profile," "family stability" and "future outcomes." No social worker had ever given spit about Reed when his old man was beating the hell out of him. Now, when it was too damn late to do anything but make trouble, some do-gooding social worker was sticking her nose into his business.

When he got to the recommendation section, he swore low and very succinctly.

"Reed?"

He slammed the report onto the table. "Damn it! They can't take her away from me."

"What does it say, Reed?"

"That damn woman is recommending Betina be removed from the household until such time as the criminal charges against you are resolved."

"Dear God..." Her eyes wide, Ann looked at him wildly. "It's my fault. Oh, Reed, I'm so sorry."

"It's not your fault. It's that narrow-minded, simpleton of a caseworker." He couldn't think of adjectives bad enough to describe what that stupid woman was doing to him. To Bets. "What gives her the right to judge you? You're a good mother. Terrific! And she's saying just because you've been accused of a penny-ante crime, you're not fit!''

"Not fit? Dear heaven, what else is going to go wrong?"

He plowed his fingers through his hair. "I'll take Bets away, that's what I'll do. We'll start over someplace else. But I won't let them take her away, damn it! I won't."

"You can't leave your home, Reed." Her voice trembled and her eyes glistened. "You know you can't raise Bets on the road. You said so yourself."

"So what other choice do I have?"

"*I'm* the problem, not you. That means I'm the one who has to go." Tears welled in her eyes like waves on an emerald sea.

He stared at her incredulously. "What are you talking about?"

"An annulment."

Her words hit him like a punch to the solar plexus, driving the wind from him. "It's too soon." He couldn't lose Ann yet. He wasn't ready to let her go. He'd thought she'd stay until the adoption was final. It could have been months. Now some cretin social worker had messed up everything. *Everything*.

"Think about it, Reed. You married me because of my impeccable reputation. Now that's a joke. But nobody's laughing. I've been arrested, lost my job. Because of my father, I came close to causing you to lose the ranch. If you weren't stuck with me, the social worker would have approved your request to adopt Bets."

"No. She would have looked under some other

damn rock and come up with a reason to turn me down. That's the way those people think.''

"She's trying to do her job.''

"The hell she is.'' Restless frustration drove Reed across the kitchen. He ran water into a glass, drank half the contents in single gulp then slammed the glass down on the counter, nearly shattering it. He'd quenched his thirst but he hadn't managed to wash the bitter taste of failure out of his mouth. *He'd promised Betsy and now they were going to take her baby away from him.*

He sensed Ann coming up behind him, and she placed her hand on his back in a caress as soft as a whisper. He wanted to turn around, pull her into his arms, bury his face in her hair and inhale her womanly scent. But he couldn't do that. Right now it would hurt too much because she was going to leave him, too. He'd known it wouldn't last. So why did he care so much?

"Maybe Marvin Hutch can do something,'' Ann said. "Get a court order to halt the proceedings. That would buy you some time.''

"Yeah, maybe.'' He watched as a car raised a plume of dust on the long dirt drive that led to the ranch house. A stranger coming. Maybe another social worker coming to get Bets. Frustration burned in Reed's gut. Betsy should have found somebody else to give her kid to. He could have told her he was a loser. His old man had said so more than once.

His mother hadn't even thought he was good enough to take him with her when she hightailed it outta here.

The car stopped short of the house as if the driver was afraid to get too close. A woman got out and stood by the vehicle. If she'd come to get Bets, what the hell was she waiting for? Maybe it was the mutt's yammering that had her hesitating to go too far from the safety of her car.

Reed frowned and squinted. The woman had golden-brown hair, and he watched in fascination as she gave her head a little toss and flipped her long hair back behind her shoulder, a nervous gesture he knew was totally unconscious.

He turned to Ann, relief twitching his lips into a near smile. "Looks like you've got company, sugar."

She blinked as though she'd been fighting her own fears as hard as he'd been struggling against his. "Now? Who?" She glanced out the window.

"Your twin."

Chapter Twelve

It was like looking in a mirror.

The stranger's hair was the same color as Ann's, cut the same length with the same natural curl at the ends. Her eyebrows arched at the same shallow angle and her eyes were the same odd shade that drifted beyond hazel into green. She was even wearing the same shade of lip gloss. Ann kept thinking if she moved, the image would move in unison with her.

"Uncanny, isn't it?" the woman said, once Arnold had quieted his barking. Her voice was a little husky, and Ann wondered if she sounded the same to others.

"Amazing." Ann stepped off the porch and walked toward her…sister. Her mind nearly balked at the unfamiliar connection. "You're Jodie Sutherland?"

"That's what my folks called me—most of the time." Her voice held a cautious note.

"We were looking for you."

"I gathered as much. My neighbor said we were dead ringers for each other. She wasn't kidding."

"No one at the apartment complex admitted they knew you."

"They were afraid I was in trouble."

Ann took a deep breath. "You are."

The stranger looked like she was about to bolt. "Look, we might look alike but I don't owe you—"

"You wrote two bad checks and I got blamed for them. It cost me my job, the county is suing me for welfare fraud, and this whole mess might cost my husband the baby he wants to adopt."

Ann's mirror image looked up at Reed, who was standing on the porch behind her. "At least you've got good taste, honey. That man is one hunky cowboy."

A fierce surge of possessiveness swept through Ann. "He's *my* cowboy," she hissed only loud enough for the woman to hear.

Jodie Sutherland tipped back her head. The laugh that escaped her throat was full and round, inviting others to join in the joke. "Honey, I don't want your man. I've got plenty of troubles all on my own."

Reed said, "Why don't you invite her in, Ann? You two ought to have a lot to talk about."

Her expression closing down, Jodie shot a glance into her car, a vintage compact with a fair share of dings and scratches. "I've got my boy with me."

"Bring him, too," Reed offered. "Unless he'd rather take a little ride on my horse. Fiero could use some exercise. A couple of trips around the corral wouldn't hurt." He walked down the steps to stand beside Ann.

"Can I, Mom? Can I?" the child in the car pleaded.

Ann's heart responded to the child's excitement. Given the poverty in which he'd apparently been raised, he'd probably had few chances to even see a ranch, much less ride a horse.

"Reed is very good with children," she assured Jodie. "He'll take good care of the boy."

"His name is Harley." She opened the car door. "He's six."

A slender, blond youngster with his hair cut in a Dutch bob sprang from the car. "I'm almost seven, Mom."

"That's right, sweet cakes, only six months to go." She smiled in a thoroughly maternal way as she cupped the back of her son's head. "Now you listen to what the man says, you hear? Try not to get into too much trouble."

"I'll be good, Mom." He dashed to Reed's side and looked up expectantly. "Have you really got a horse, mister?"

"Sure do, kid. A whole bunch of white-faced, ugly steers, too. This is a working cattle ranch."

"Wow! I used to live on a farm but we didn't have no horse."

Ann met and matched Jodie's smile as Reed strolled toward the barn, the boy skipping beside him and the dog trotting along. "Would you like some coffee?"

"Sure, if it isn't too much trouble."

Ann thought a pot of coffee would be a worthwhile exchange in order to have her growing curiosity satisfied.

REED GAVE THE WOMEN plenty of time to get acquainted, letting the kid ride Fiero bareback while he led the horse around the corral. He figured if Ann and her newly discovered sister came to blows, one of them would scream loud enough for him to come running. Mostly he assumed they'd dance around each other for a while and then get down to woman talk. Ann would probably know Jodie's entire life history within sixty minutes, and vice versa. He'd get an earful later.

Then they could get down to the business of clearing Ann's name.

After a few laps of the corral, he got Harley off the horse and had him stand safely outside the fence to feed Fiero a carrot or two.

"Come on, short stuff," he called to the boy when he thought enough time had passed for the women to have shared their entire biographies. "Let's go see if my wife and your mom have had their fill of gabbing yet."

He grinned at Reed. "She don't ever get tired of talking."

"Seems to me most women are like that." Though Ann, he'd noticed, didn't run off at the mouth like some he'd met. She could handle silence, even seemed to enjoy it from time to time. He liked that in a woman. One of the best things about living on a ranch was the quiet that seeped into your bones.

He wouldn't want a woman around who talked all the time. Ann was easy on a man's nerves.

Hell on his libido, though, particularly knowing she wasn't going to stay long. She was already talking about an annulment. God, that hurt. Theirs would be the world's shortest marriage on record.

And that's exactly the deal he'd made—signed, sealed and very nearly delivered since Jodie Sutherland had showed up. When the truth was known, the damn caseworker would approve Bets's adoption and Ann would be outta here. Tough luck for ol' Reed if he wanted things different.

Which he didn't, he told himself as he opened the back door to the house. With a ranch to run and Bets to take care of, he had plenty on his plate. Anybody could see he wasn't the marrying kind—not for the long haul, anyway.

As he expected, the women were in the kitchen.

Though they looked alike there were differences, too. Instead of being studiously mellow like Ann, her sister had flirty eyes that sparkled with amusement even when faced with near disaster, he suspected. She dressed differently, too. Her look announced high fashion was way down on her priority list. With her, casual worked. She wore a loosely fitting tunic top with a beaded necklace and a long broomstick skirt that nearly reached her ankles. Good-looking but lacking Ann's classic touch.

Reed had a fondness for classy.

"Hey, Mom." Harley shot past Reed into the kitchen. "I rode the horse all by myself, and I got to feed him carrots and stuff! He's got really funny lips and *big* teeth.''

She pulled her son to her for a hug. ''I hope you thanked Mr. Drummond for letting you ride his horse.''

''Oh, yeah. Sure. Thanks, mister,'' he said belatedly.

Ann reached out for Reed almost as if she wanted to give him a hug, too. Her cheeks glowed with excitement, and she had Bets in her lap, jiggling her gently.

''You won't believe how much Jodie and I are alike,'' Ann said effusively. ''She loves root beer instead of Coke and clam linguine is her favorite pasta. I haven't made that for you yet, have I?''

''That's okay. I'm more a steak-and-potatoes type.''

''She knew she was adopted. Her parents told her. But they didn't say anything about there being two of us.''

''Thinking there was another one like me probably would have given my folks a cardiac,'' Jodie said with a laugh. ''I wasn't exactly the perfect child.''

''Neither was I.'' Ann closed her hand around Reed's, squeezing slightly as if reminding him her one fling on the wild side had left her wounded, too.

Unused to displays of affection in front of others, even a simple holding of hands, he slipped free of Ann's grasp and went to the counter to pour himself a cup of coffee.

''She and Harley have had a really hard time of

it since his father died and they moved out of the commune.''

Reed slid Jodie a questioning look. "Commune?''

She shrugged. "Alex and I laughed about being late-blooming flower children. We raised organic vegetables.''

"My dad was the leader of the whole place,'' said Harley, "but then he fell off a tractor and bonked his head real hard.''

"That's tough,'' Reed said sympathetically. The coffee was hot and rich, just the way he liked it. He wondered if he'd ever told Ann that's what he wanted—or if she had simply sensed his preferences.

"Anyway,'' Ann said, "Jodie applied for welfare when she decided to live on the outside after the commune went broke, but there were delays. She had trouble getting a job. One thing led to another.''

"Honestly, I don't make it a practice to write bad checks. Things just got, well, a little tight there for a while.''

"I've told Jodie we'll cover the bad checks she wrote and get Marvin Hutch to handle her case. He was pretty sure the storekeeper would drop the charges if he got his money.''

Reed winced at the expense, but it would be worth it to get this mess cleared up. And he vowed he'd somehow come up with the cash himself, not use Ann's from her mortgaged house.

"I'll pay you back,'' Jodie promised. "I've got a job now at a health food store. It isn't much but at least I'm not on welfare anymore, and we've got a decent roof over our heads."

"That's why she moved," Ann told him. "But it's still only a one-bedroom apartment." She lifted Bets and put her on her shoulder. Milky drool edged out of the baby's mouth, and Reed smiled.

"Here, let me take her." Reed reached for the baby.

"We're getting by." Jodie shoved her hair back behind her shoulder and lifted her chin.

Reed suspected the twins shared a common bond of stubbornness. "Maybe we ought to let Fuentes know you're in the clear," he suggested to Ann.

"You're probably—"

Someone banged on the back door. Without waiting for a response, Jason burst into the house.

"Hey, Miz Forrester...I mean Mrs. Drum—" He came to an abrupt halt in the kitchen. His gaze shot from Jodie to Ann and back again. "Way cool! I didn't know you had a twin."

Ann smiled at the youngster's wide-eyed expression and realized with a lurch that she missed seeing her students, however much the adolescents made a concerted effort to drive her crazy. "Neither did I until recently."

"No fooling?" He shuffled from one foot to the other, obviously not quite sure what to make of the situation.

"You can go clean out Fiero's stall, if you want," Reed said.

"Yeah, okay. But that's not why I come up here—"

"Came," Ann automatically corrected.

"Right. Came. I mean, I came to work but there's something else, too. Something important."

Standing, Ann took Jason by the shoulder. "What is it? Are you in trouble? Is it something about your mother? Your foster home?"

"Naw. Nothing like that." He gave her a devilish grin not unlike Reed's patented rogue smile.

By the time Jason was fifteen he'd be a lady-killer, Ann thought with a silent groan. "Then what?"

"There's gonna be a demonstration at school tomorrow."

"Demonstration?" she echoed.

"Yeah, you know, like a strike. The kids are gonna skip class and picket. So are some of the teachers. I got their names on a petition, see?" He pulled a wad of papers from his back pocket. "That stupid school board ain't gonna know what hit 'em when we get done with 'em."

"What on earth are you talking about?"

"It's how they fired you, that's what." All fury and bluster, Jason stuck out his chest and stood a little taller than he ever had before. "It's not right what they did to you. You haven't been convicted of nothin'."

"Anything."

"And they ought to do innocent until proven guilty, right?"

"Absolutely," Reed agreed.

"So we're gonna picket."

"Jason Hilary!" She cupped his chin, forcing him

to look at her. "What happened? Did the substitute give you a homework assignment that was too tough for you to handle?"

"Aw, geez no, Miz Forrester. She doesn't know squat about math. She even messed up on a square root problem a baby could've solved. I want you back, is all. I mean, all us kids do."

A rush of love nearly undid Ann. She'd been on an emotional roller coaster for weeks. Now a smart-alecky adolescent was about to turn her into a blubbering female whose hormones were clearly on the rampage. Dear heaven, of all the youngsters in school it was the bad boys like Jason who tugged at her heart. More than once she'd wanted to hug him, to bring him home and keep him safe.

"So you organized a strike of the kids?" She struggled to keep the quaver of emotion from her voice.

"It wasn't so hard. Mr. Dunlap, like, has his head in the sand."

Ann could certainly appreciate that, though she couldn't approve Jason's actions. "Well, you're just going to have to stop the strike. Children belong in—"

"I can't, Miz Forr—Drummond. If you want it stopped, do it yourself." Whirling, he marched out of the house the way he'd come in.

"Wait, Jason. I'm sorry—"

"I'd say that young man has a serious crush on you," Jodie said as the back door slammed.

"He's at an impressionable age," Ann conceded. "But a strike? I don't know what—"

"I think it's a great idea." Leaning against the counter with Bets cuddled to his chest, Reed had lulled the baby to sleep. "A strike will embarrass the hell out of the school board."

"You and Jason are two of a kind," Ann muttered, secretly pleased these two particular males had stuck up for her against the accusations of others. In Jason's case, however, he'd left her with a predicament she would have to rectify—first thing tomorrow morning. She couldn't have her students cutting classes out of a misguided sense of loyalty to her, though she loved them for the thought.

Reed's lips slid into an easy smile. "Yeah, we're both suckers for innocent women."

The warm glow of love that Jason had kindled by being her youthful champion heated considerably under Reed's intense scrutiny and turned into something far more adult.

"I'm going to put Bets down," Reed said. "Then I'll call Hutch to get the ball rolling for charges to be dropped against you and get Jodie off the hook. Then I'll talk to that fool social worker."

Things didn't work out the way Reed had hoped. Marvin Hutch was gone for the day and Clarisa Fipp was "in the field" and wouldn't be in the office until the following morning.

Frustrated, he left terse messages for both of them.

ANN'S ALREADY NERVOUS stomach jumped, and she groaned when she discovered a near-riot going on at the school the next morning.

Kids were milling in looping circles in front of the entrance, waving an assortment of hand-lettered Unfair to Mrs. Drummond picket signs while the school band blared a discordant rendition of a Sousa march. Meanwhile, a photographer from the *Mar del Oro Press Enterprise* snapped pictures for the next edition of the MOPE.

As Reed helped her out of the truck, a wildly cheering throng including parents and very nearly all of the school faculty greeted her. Her heart swelled with affection for every one of them.

"Looks like Jason really started something," Reed said under his breath. "Nothing like a rebel with a cause."

"Three cheers for Mrs. Drummond!" the students shouted

"Hip, hip, hooray!" came the echo.

Ann winced as the camera flash went off in her face.

As difficult as it was to retain her composure, she searched the crowd for Jason to help her bring this demonstration to a halt. When she spotted him, he shot her a youthful, self-satisfied grin. It was all she could do not to laugh.

If nothing else, it appeared Jason had discovered his innate leadership abilities and put them to work—however inappropriately.

Mr. Dunlap came running out from the administration building. "You have to stop the children, Ms. Forr—Drummond. They're refusing to go to class. And my phone's been ringing off the hook since I stepped in my office this morning." Red-faced, he tried to catch his breath. "The parents are upset and the school board has rescinded their previous order. You really must control—" His eyes widened and his mouth hung open as Jodie Sutherland joined Ann on the sidewalk. "Wh-who's she?" he stammered.

"Mr. Dunlap, I'd like you to meet my twin sister, Jodie Sutherland, who is no more of a hardened criminal than I am."

Apparently someone had called the cops because the police chief's cruiser roared up to the front of the school, lights flashing.

"Maybe I shouldn't have come," Jodie said, taking a step back.

"It'll be all right," Ann assured her, hoping that was the truth. Being falsely judged once herself, she could understand her twin's caution. She'd been pleased when Jodie had agreed to meet her here this morning. They were scheduled to go from here to meet Marvin Hutch at the police station to clear up both the bad checks and Ann's arrest. But she hadn't expected Johnny Fuentes to show up at the school.

Shoving his nightstick into a belt loop, he ignored the jostling students and strolled in Ann's direction. The chanting youngsters enthusiastically increased their volume by several decibels.

"My boy's in the car. If that cop arrests me—"

"He'll have five hundred rioting students on his hands and a fair number of adults. Trust me. Everything's going to be fine."

Reed ambled up to join them, his rugged cowboy image not damaged in the least by the baby he carried in a blue denim sling. He thumbed his Stetson up on his forehead and grinned at the chaotic scene.

"Looks like you're running for Congress or something," he said.

Johnny halted a few feet from Ann. Amusement sparking in his dark eyes, he glanced from her to Jodie. A smile curled his lips. "Looks like you were right, Ann. What we've got here is a case of mistaken identity. Either that or I'm developing a bad case of double vision in my old age."

"My twin, Jodie Sutherland," Ann provided. "Our attorney is going to work things out. After we're through here, we're meeting him at the station."

"Chief, you have to do something about these students," Mr. Dunlap pleaded. The circle of youngsters pressed in more closely around them. The sound of their chants was deafening.

"With this many kids, I'll have to call for backup," Johnny said easily. "Might take them a while to get here."

The principal looked around in rising panic. "Can't you see they're out of control? Jason Hilary is behind this. I know he is. He's always been a troublemaker."

"He hasn't been in trouble for weeks, Mr. Dunlap," Ann said in the boy's defense. "Not since Reed began mentoring him."

"Then it was only a matter of time before he got into even bigger mischief," the principal insisted.

"Why don't you tell 'em Ann's back on the payroll," Reed suggested mildly. "That would put a halt to their holiday."

"Sounds like a good plan to me," Johnny agreed.

Dunlap sputtered something about bowing to blackmail.

At the back of the crowd, a commotion arose. The plump figure of Clarisa Fipp pushed her way through the students. She planted her fists on her broad hips.

"Officer, I need your help." She drew several deep breaths before she spoke again. "I have reason to believe Mr. and Mrs. Drummond are planning to kidnap that baby and remove her from the county's jurisdiction."

Reed glowered at the social worker. "She doesn't belong to the damn county. Bets is mine."

"Your message to my secretary made it clear you were not going to comply with the county's order to relinquish the child—"

"You've got that damn straight."

"When I didn't find you at the ranch, I called the police. Dispatch sent me here to find the chief."

Ann rolled her eyes. Matters were indeed getting out of hand.

She raised her hand, a signal her students recognized as an order for them to be quiet. The adults had less understanding of the signal as Ms. Fipp and Mr. Dunlap kept demanding the chief of police resolve of their respective problems.

Finally, the students were silenced and the adults sputtered to a stop.

"I want to thank you all for your support and encouragement,'' Ann said when she had everyone's attention, speaking loudly enough to be heard at the back of the crowd. "Mr. Dunlap has informed me that I will be back in the classroom on Monday morning.''

The students cheered.

"I believe it would be best if you resume teaching today, Mrs. Drum—"

"I'm taking the day off today—personal business,'' she told him in no uncertain terms. To the gathered crowd she said, ''I believe I heard the first bell some time ago. All of you belong in your classrooms, not here.'' She spotted Marcy McCullough among the onlooking faculty members. "The teachers, too,'' she said with a smile.

Grumbling good-naturedly that the fun was over, the crowd began to disperse, the teachers leading the way.

"I suggest the rest of us adjourn to Mr. Dunlap's office,'' Ann said to the remaining characters in this impromptu farce. "I'm sure he won't mind us using it to get some of these other misunderstandings resolved.''

Although Clarisa didn't seem thrilled at the prospect of going anywhere with Reed, who was doing his tough-cowboy imitation, Ann got everyone inside and seated around a table.

Johnny quickly announced he'd be dropping all charges against Ann and felt there would be no need to file any against Jodie if the bad checks were covered. Reed promised they would be.

All eyes then turned to Clarisa.

She flushed. "Well, yes, under the circumstances, I suppose I can safely recommend Mr. and Mrs. Drummond be granted guardianship of Betina Shoemaker pending final adoption approval. They both appear to be devoted parents."

Reed visibly relaxed.

Ann wasn't quite so relieved, and her nervous stomach registered another tumble.

As the meeting broke up, she and Reed headed for his truck. He sighed. "Thank God that's over."

"You got what you wanted."

He smiled at the baby cuddled in his arms. "I did, didn't I? Thanks to your help."

Ann could only hope Reed achieving his goal didn't signal the end of her marriage, too.

Chapter Thirteen

Reed popped the cork on the champagne bottle.

Ann jumped and turned from her contemplation of the cowboy miniature on the fireplace mantel. "I didn't hear you come in."

"Since you got Bets down and Fiero is set for the night, I figured this was a good time to celebrate." Not knowing how long Ann would stay, Reed couldn't be sure there'd *ever* be another time. He wanted this one to count.

She arched a curious eyebrow. "And you just happened to have a bottle of champagne on hand?"

"I had to go into town for more shingle nails this afternoon. I just *happened* to go by a liquor store."

"How fortuitous."

"I thought so." He smiled as he poured wine into the glasses he'd brought from the kitchen. Not exactly crystal goblets but they'd do. He set the bottle on the end table next to the couch and handed Ann one of the glasses. "Here's to beating the bureaucrats."

Her eyes sparkling more than the champagne, she

touched the rim of her glass to his. "I'm not sure we beat anything. More like they finally were forced to see the truth."

"Having your twin show up was pretty damn convincing, all right."

"And having a boy like Jason on my side certainly makes an impression." She laughed. "I swear I didn't know whether to laugh or cry or turn him over my knee and give him a good spanking. Or better yet, adopt that youngster and give him the kind of home he deserves."

"Ms. Fipp would probably flip out if we tried that," he said with a low-throated chuckle.

They both sipped from their glasses. Reed could barely taste the fruity liquid. Instead he wanted to taste Ann. All day he'd been thinking, one last time and then he'd be able to let her go—let her get the annulment she'd talked about. Now he wasn't so sure.

She had her hair pulled back in a loose pony tail and some of the strands had escaped to lie against her cheek. With his fingertip, he smoothed the wayward strands back behind her ear. Her eyes flared and she drew in a soft breath. Reed's body reacted with its own tightening low in his groin. He inhaled her scent, wildflowers and something difficult to define that was uniquely her own.

"How 'bout a fire?" he asked, his voice thick and husky. In his fantasies, he'd pictured Ann naked and golden in the firelight while he made love to her. He couldn't wait till winter for that dream to come true. She'd be gone by then, and he fought the desolate sense of loneliness that nearly swamped him at the thought.

"I'd like a fire." She held her glass with both hands, her delicate fingers curling around the tumbler the way Reed wanted them to curl around him. She brought the champagne to her lips again, sipping slowly. "One of the reasons I bought my house in town was because it has a fireplace."

He gritted his teeth against the ache that rose from deep in his jeans. "It can get pretty damp and cold around here in the winter."

"Yes, I know. A fire is cozy."

Cozy wasn't exactly what he had in mind as he set his glass aside and knelt to lay the logs on the grate. He lit a match to the newspapers he'd stuffed in the cracks, but the flames that shot up couldn't compare to the sensual fire that was burning in his gut. *One last time,* he told himself.

Still kneeling, he extended his hand to her. She took it, joining him on the carpet in front of the fire. They leaned back against the couch, and she set her glass aside to watch the flames coil up the chimney. The sharp scent of woodsmoke crept into the room as the log caught.

"I still can hardly believe I have a twin. I think she and I are going to become friends."

"It figures you'd have a lot in common." He loved when Ann wore her hair back, baring the vulnerable column of her neck. Lightly, he stroked the soft, downy skin at her nape.

"I..." Her voice caught. "I like Harley, too. He seems very... Reed?"

"Hmm?" Leaning closer, he brushed his lips to the juncture of her neck and shoulder.

"Are you...ah..." A fine shudder went through her. "Seducing me?"

"That's my plan." *One last time.*

"How nice." A tiny smile quivered at the corners of her lips.

He found her ear and circled the delicate shell with his tongue, heat spiralling through him as he did. "Very nice."

With a sigh, her head fell back, giving him easy access to the sweet hollow of her throat. "You do this very well," she murmured.

"I have a willing subject." Only his own body was betraying him. He wanted this to last, to linger over every silky bit of Ann so the memories would be embedded in his psyche. As he undressed her, slipping her shirt off over her head and removing her bra, he gave particular attention to the rosy nipples she thrust up at him, tasting their creamy flavor, memorizing the beaded texture.

Her breathing deepened. When he looked at her, her eyes had fluttered closed, her mouth was open and a faint glow of pleasure colored her cheeks. Fierce, masculine pride shot through him at her erotic response to his ministrations.

Once he had tried to deny himself the pleasure of this fiercely sexual woman. In the future he'd have to do so again. But for now she was his—in this minute, in this place, he would have her. Later he'd lock away the memories and bring them out only when he was feeling particularly strong.

"Reed..." Moaning, she twisted her hips and tried to slip her slacks off. "Too many clothes. Help me."

"My pleasure."

In minutes their clothing had been cast aside and Ann was stretched out on the floor beside Reed, naked and beautiful. He caressed the flatness of her stomach, kissed the indentation of her belly button and slid his hand through the golden-brown curls that protected her secret heat. The striking contrast between his tanned skin and her fair complexion was deeply erotic. When he dipped his fingers lower, she bucked against him.

"Oh, Reed..."

"My sweet sugar-Annie." He tasted her heat, laved it until she arched and cried out his name, her whole body shuddering. *His* name, by damn. He never wanted her to forget it.

Then he knelt between her legs, spread them and invaded her with tender savagery, taking them both where they would never go again. He watched her, the golden firelight dancing across her face as she reached toward her peak. He plunged into her again, this time letting her draw him ever more fully inside. The wood crackled in the fireplace, sending up sparks. The tension in him rose to an unbearable pitch then exploded in final release as her body pulsed around him.

He stayed inside her as long as he could. Resting on his forearms, he kept his weight from crushing her. But drained of strength and hope, a deep melancholy overtook him, and he finally had to roll away. He knew he had to be the one to call an end to what he'd started only weeks ago. If he allowed her to walk away first, Reed's pain would be too great to endure. If he was going to survive, he'd have to protect himself.

"We'll talk to Marvin Hutch next week," Reed said. Only a tiny flame continued to lick at the charred log in the fireplace. "He'll know how to go about getting us an annulment."

Blinking, Ann came out of her sensual haze in a blaze of disappointment and pain that quickly turned to fury.

"Hutch will do what?" she repeated, doing all she could not to let her voice rise to a screech.

"Arrange our annulment."

She scooted away from Reed so she wouldn't pound him into oblivion with her fists. With the adrenaline surging through her veins, she'd have the strength to kill him if she let herself go. "You make the most incredible love to me I've ever experienced and two minutes later you're talking annulment? I don't believe you!"

"It's what we agreed to. There's no rush, of course."

"*No rush?*" she mocked. "I'll show you rush."

Scrambling to her feet, she snatched up her clothes, which were scattered on the floor near the couch. She couldn't do this. She couldn't give her heart to a man and then allow him to toss it back in her face.

She'd thought—she'd *believed*—Reed loved her, even when he hadn't said the words. Hadn't he just showed her how much he cared? It was more than lust, damn it! He'd stuck with her when she'd been arrested, when being married to her might have cost him custody of Betina. Now he was ready to toss her—and their love—out on her metaphorical ear.

She'd been lying to herself. The worst kind of fool. He'd said from the beginning that marriage stinks. That's what she should have believed.

No rush, he'd said. The hell with it! And him!

She wasn't going to stay around here waiting for a lightning bolt to strike him and bring the arrogant cowboy to his senses. If he was too dense to believe they could have a life together, then so be it. She would not stay one second longer with a man who didn't recognize and respond to love when it hit him right smack between the eyes.

With her gone, maybe he'd recognize what he'd lost—what they'd both lost.

Belatedly, Reed came to his feet. "What are you doing?"

"I'm leaving you. What does it look like?" Hugging her clothing to her chest, her butt as naked as the day she was born, she marched out of the living room and down the hall. In the bedroom she yanked her suitcase out of the back of the closet.

"You don't have to leave right now," Reed said from the doorway. He didn't have anything more on than she did.

"You've had your last roll in the hay with me, Reed Drummond, unless you can give me a damn good reason to stay."

"It's getting late. You shouldn't be out driving—"

"Not good enough, Drummond." She opened a drawer, grabbed an armload of undies and dropped them into the suitcase. "I've been driving after dark since before you came along. I think I can still manage."

"Come on, sugar. Be reasonable. You're upset—"

"How clever of you to notice." She dragged armfuls of clothes out of the closet. One by one, she tossed aside the hangers and crammed the dresses and skirts into the suitcase, not caring about the mess they'd be in by the time she unpacked them. All she wanted to do was get out of here. Get away from Reed. Lick the wounds to her pride. It didn't pay to love a man who didn't know how to love in return.

Except he knew how to love Bets, Ann thought, with a painful twist in her chest. And so did she. If Ann left, for the second time she'd be losing a child she'd come to love. She'd be leaving behind another big chunk of her heart.

A lump formed in her throat and she swallowed it down. She had no more right to Bets than she did to Reed.

She had to retreat now while she still had something of herself left to hang on to.

To get dressed, she had to rummage through the suitcase again for clothes she'd just stuffed in there—the ones Reed had removed with such seductive skill less than an hour ago. Though her vision was blurred, she noted Reed had found some clothes to put on, too. She wished to high heaven he'd learn to button his shirt. He was too damn sexy for any woman's peace of mind with his broad chest on display.

Not that she cared at the moment. Surely her fury, her humiliation, had squelched any resemblance of sexual attraction she might feel for Reed.

Yeah, right. In my dreams!

But she'd get over him. Broken hearts mended, or so she'd been told. And sex, in general, was seriously overrated—except when performed by a master craftsman. Like Reed.

She slammed her suitcase closed and zipped it shut. Or tried to. A summer top and one of her skirts was sticking out the side. She didn't give a damn.

"You don't have to do this," Reed said.

He was doing his silent cowboy imitation, she realized, the tough guy, the one without a heart. At least not a heart Ann could touch.

She hefted the suitcase off the bed. "I'd like to drop by to see Bets once in a while." Ann couldn't face that particular goodbye right now. She needed a reprieve and maybe some glimmer of hope for the future.

Reed's eyes were dark and unreadable, his brows drawn low. "Sure. No problem."

"Great. I'll call first." Snatching up her purse from the dresser, she shoved past him out the bedroom door. Her throat was tight with tears as she walked by Bets's bedroom, the nightlight glowing a soft yellow. Reed had only loaned her his baby. Now Bets belonged to him again.

Shoving out the front door, she could barely see through her tears well enough to get down the porch steps.

Arnold came running, no doubt surprised by all the activity this late at night.

"Take care of him, boy. Bets, too." She ruffled his long fur and scratched him behind his ears. "And if he gives you a hard time, you come find me, you hear? I love..." She walked away because her throat had closed on the emotional lump that had formed, one that would very likely be a permanent impediment to speech.

Ann didn't know how she made it back to town and to her house. A darkness enveloped her that lasted the entire weekend. By Monday morning when she tried to eat some breakfast before leaving for school she realized why her emotional reactions had been so volatile, her tears so near the surface...and her stomach so queasy.

She was pregnant with Reed's child.

Chapter Fourteen

Reed was changing Bets's diaper when he heard the knock on the front door.

"Come in," he shouted. Closing his eyes momentarily, he tried to will the caller to be Ann. He'd had a lousy weekend and he didn't think Monday was going to be much better. He'd burned the damn coffeepot dry and there hadn't been any milk for his cereal. Damned if he hadn't gotten used to Ann fixing him bacon and eggs or pancakes for breakfast. Worse, Bets had been fussy since Saturday as if she knew something was wrong, and he hadn't been getting more than two hours of sleep at a time.

God, he'd missed Ann when he'd gotten back into that cold, lonely bed.

More than once in the past two days Reed had made it as far as his truck, planning to drive down the hill to her house and drag her back to the ranch, back into his life.

But they'd agreed to only a temporary arrangement. She'd fulfilled her part of the bargain. He had to let her go. He didn't have to like it.

With a spring in her step, Eleanor Forrester pranced into the baby's room. "Good morning, Reed. How's our little lamb today?"

He tried to hide his disappointment that it wasn't Ann, but her mother who'd showed up. He caught the fastening on the diaper and pulled it tight. "I didn't expect to see you this morning," he said to Eleanor.

"I heard in town Ann would be going back to work today. I assumed you'd want me—"

"She's not here."

"Ann's not? You mean, she's already left for—"

"She moved out Friday night. I assume she's at her own place." A house she'd mortgaged to the hilt to pay off a loan for Reed so he could keep his ranch. Well, he'd have to make sure that arrangement had been reversed. He didn't want to owe Ann anything. That hadn't been part of the deal. And for Bets's sake, he wanted the title to the land free and clear. It was the one legacy he could give her.

"Ann didn't call me. Usually, if there's a problem..." Frowning, Eleanor shook her head, evidently surprised by the news. "You two had a fight?"

"Something like that." He lifted Bets to his shoulder, finding her much more sweet-smelling now than she had been minutes ago. "You don't have to stay."

She reached out to touch Bets's cheek. "Seems to me I agreed to baby-sit this little lamb, not get embroiled in my daughter's marital problems. I'm sure you two will work things out."

"I'm not quite that confident." Especially since he'd practically shoved her out the door. Better that than let her walk out on her own. A man had to protect his macho image, right? And his fool ego.

"Hmm." She took Bets from him and kissed her on the cheek. "My daughter can be a stubborn one, can't she? Takes after her father, I suppose." She flushed, realizing as an adopted child, genetics was not part of the equation. "Well, learned it from him, at any rate. You know, we've offered Jodie Sutherland the use of the guest cottage on the back of our property. She and her son need somewhere safer to stay."

"You've seen her?"

"Richard and I drove over to San Luis Obispo on Saturday to meet her. We both feel so guilty. If we'd known they were twins..." Holding the baby to her shoulder, she stroked Bets's back. "Well, water under the bridge, as they say. Richard's going to try to locate a better job for her, too. She's barely making minimum wage. Such a pity. Of course, she seemed a bit hesitant about accepting Richard's help. Pride, I suppose."

"That's real nice of you, Eleanor. And Richard, too." Though Reed didn't have particularly fond feelings for a man who had tried to foreclose on his ranch without giving him a chance to succeed. "Look, under the circumstances, Ann being gone and all, you don't have to stay with Bets. But if you could for a little while, I've got some business in town."

"Oh, you go ahead, young man. Bets and I will be just fine, won't we, sweetie?"

Reed counted himself lucky Eleanor hadn't walked out on him the moment she learned Ann had left. Eventually he'd have to find somebody else. She wouldn't stick around if Ann wasn't involved. But for now, Eleanor was a godsend. He couldn't shove her away—like he had Ann, he thought grimly. Doing business with a baby in tow was damn difficult.

He'd shoved a lot of people out of his life over the years. He'd even tried to with Betsy and Tommy. He was used to being alone. Life was easier without attachments.

Reed left Bets with Eleanor, did his morning chores around the ranch, and was at the bank in town when the doors opened. He went directly to David Emery.

"I want to check on my line of credit." Reed took a chair opposite the spit-and-polish bank manager and placed his hat on the chair next to him. In contrast to Emery's suit and carefully knotted tie, Reed was wearing his work jeans and an old blue shirt.

"Of course. Reed Drummond, isn't it?"

"You got it."

Emery gave him a faint smile. "Your father-in-law apparently overstepped his bounds. You've been issued a new line of credit."

"New? What happened to the old one?"

"Ann...that is, your wife paid off the balance owed."

Reed bristled at Emery's too-familiar reference to Ann. "I want the loan *un*paid off."

"Oh?" His brows arched slightly. "I'm not sure—"

"Ann and I are splitting, okay? Our prenuptial says she doesn't have any financial interest in my ranch, and I want it to stay that way."

"Really? Ann seems like such a charming woman, I'm surprised your marriage was so brief." Emery's cool gleam of masculine interest grated on Reed. If they'd been in a bar and he'd looked at Ann that way, Reed would have smashed the guy in the face.

"It happens." It probably wouldn't have happened to a guy like Emery, though. He was as smooth as Teflon. Some women went for men like that, particularly classy women like Ann. Now that Reed was out of the picture, Emery would have a clear field if he wanted to hit on Ann. Reed wouldn't be able to stop him. And damn it, he shouldn't care. But he did. His fingers ached from clenching them into fists.

"Yes, I suppose that's unfortunate, but true. I'll have to review our procedures to determine the most expeditious way of reversing the previous arrangement. It may take me a day or two to get everything in order."

"Just see that's it done." Picking up his hat, Reed stood.

Emery followed suit. "I may have to contact Ann...your wife, to determine how she would like us proceed."

"Yeah, I'll just bet you'll have to." Reed figured Emery would have a helluva lot more on his mind than a bank loan.

ANN'S STOMACH ROILED. The science class down the hall was doing something awful and the rotten-egg smell had drifted into her classroom. Normally that sort of thing didn't bother her much. It did now.

Odd smells had bothered her the last time she'd been pregnant too. Early morning queasiness had plagued her almost from the day she'd conceived— until she'd lost the baby.

Instinctively, her hand slid across her belly. Dear heaven, she didn't want to lose Reed's child.

"Miz Drummond, the substitute didn't explain all this *X-Y* axis stuff. I don't get it."

Ann would have to tell Reed about the baby, but not just yet. Though he might deny he was the most responsible man in the world—a rolling stone, he'd say, who thought marriage stank—he'd want to do the "right" thing by her and their baby. Ann didn't want a marriage based on obligation.

She wanted one based on love.

"Miz Drummond, how can you get minus zero to add up to anything? This is dumb."

She blinked and looked around the classroom. The students were looking at her as if she'd grown a second head. Or she was green around the gills. Which was undoubtedly true. That smell...

"Stay in your seats. I'll be right—" Her hand covering her mouth, she made a dash for the door and the teachers' lounge.

JASON DRAGGED a bundle of shingles to the spot where Reed was squatting on the roof, hammer in hand. The afternoon sun beat down on him. Under his hatband, he could feel the sweat rising. His palms were damp with it, his shirt sticking to his back.

"So how come she moved out?" Jason asked.

"None of your business, kid."

"You messed up, didn't you?"

"I told you—" The hammer struck Reed's thumb, and he swore. "Just do your work and quit asking so damn many questions."

"Maybe it's just her hormones are screwed up."

Reed cut him a look. "Why would you say a dumb thing like that?"

"'Cause she's upchucking all over the place, that's why."

The hammer froze in midair. "She's sick?"

"Naw. She's pregnant, man. Don't you know nuthin'?"

Reed lost his balance and his feet slid out from under him. He nearly went flying over the edge of the barn roof. Only by digging his fingers and the toes of his boots into the shingles did he manage to save himself. "How'd you know she's throwing up?" he asked, after he caught his breath. With his teeth, he yanked at a splinter that had stuck in his finger.

"Man, she went running out the classroom this morning looking like she'd eaten a bunch of bad fish. Everybody saw her."

Reed's brain wouldn't accept the possibility that

the kid knew what he was talking about. He and Ann hadn't been married all that long. And he'd been careful, damn it. Most of the time. "Maybe she *had* eaten something or she's got stomach flu. Teachers get exposed to all kinds of—"

"I'm telling you, man. She was back the next period lookin' fine." Jason jutted out his chin. "That don't happen if it's the stupid flu. I've had *two* foster moms who puked every morning the whole time they were pregnant."

Damn! Could it be true? "Come on. Get yourself off this roof." He lifted the kid by the back of his shirt, hauling him to his feet.

"Hey, man, I didn't do nuthin' wrong. You can't send me home now without paying me my whole shift. It's union rules."

"You're not in any damn union. And I'm not leaving you up here on the roof by yourself where you can fall off and break your fool neck after I'm gone. I've got business in town." He half shoved him toward the ladder.

"But you'll pay me anyways?"

"I'll pay you. Now, get down the ladder before I throw you off the roof myself."

Ann would be at home now, he thought, taking only enough time to tell Eleanor he'd be gone for a while. If Ann was pregnant, her mother sure didn't know—or hadn't let on. Sure as hell, Ann would want to stay married if she was having a baby. It only made sense. After all the mess of mistaken identity, her spotless reputation had been restored.

She wouldn't want to risk losing that again. And Reed would have her back—at least for a while.

But first he had to find out if what Jason had said was true.

SHE'D WAITED all weekend for him to come to her, to come to his senses. Maybe she'd left too hastily last Friday, but she'd been too hurt and humiliated by his words to stay a moment longer.

And now he was here standing in her doorway looking worn and weary and wonderfully masculine in his sweat-dampened shirt and worn jeans. Ann wanted to leap into his arms; she wanted to cry in relief. She wanted to punch him for making her so miserable for three whole days.

"Hi," she said, opening the door more widely for him.

He didn't budge. "There's only one thing I want to know, and I want the truth."

She frowned.

"Are you pregnant?"

All the blood drained from her face. "How did you know?"

"Are you sure? We were careful—"

"Except the night after I got out of jail, if you'll recall."

He seemed to acknowledge that one critical exception when he'd finally lost the tight hold on his control.

"Were you planning to tell me anytime soon?" he asked bitterly.

"I only just realized this weekend. It's really too early—"

"It doesn't matter. I'll take your word for it. Get what you need. You're coming back home with me."

Ann dug in her mental heels. One of the youngsters at school had probably suspected what was wrong when she'd run out of the room that morning. Jason, she thought with grim certainty, knowing the youngster was more worldly-wise than most his age. He'd no doubt been the one to break the news to Reed.

"I asked you the other night to come up with a good reason for me to stay. You couldn't come up with one then. Why is now any different?"

"Damn it, because you're pregnant with my kid. What better reason could there be for us to stick it out together? At least until after the baby is born."

Time tables. Everything with this man had a time limit—a temporary arrangement—as though he couldn't bring himself to believe in forever.

She turned and walked into the living room, leaving the door open behind her. She didn't want him to see the hurt that must be apparent in her eyes. "Lots of women have babies outside the bonds of matrimony. You'll have to come up with a much better reason than that if you want me to come home with you."

"Be reasonable, sugar. You lost one baby. You don't want to lose another one. Let me take care of you."

She placed her hand on the mantel right near the

spot where the Dream Man miniature used to rest, an artifact she'd left at Reed's ranch. Her real-life cowboy had broken her heart, and now he was reminding her of one of the worst moments of her life.

"You play dirty, Drummond."

"I only want you back home with me."

"Why?"

"I told you. You're going to have my baby. Isn't that good enough?"

"No."

"Come on, sugar Annie. This isn't right."

"I want you to leave. Now."

He tried to object further but she didn't respond. Finally the silence dragged out. She heard the click of the door as he closed it behind him, then his footsteps on her walkway. Moments later she heard the truck engine start. He was gone.

She would *not* stay in a marriage without love, would not raise her child in a household without love. Reed, more than most men, ought to understand that. His loveless childhood had scarred him. She would not allow that to happen to their child.

IT TOOK REED two days to finish the roofing job. He worked on it from dawn to dusk while Eleanor babysat Bets. He wanted to be exhausted so he could sleep. All his efforts didn't do him much good. He spent most of the night staring up at the ceiling, every muscle in his body aching, missing Ann so much he thought he would go crazy.

The next afternoon Reed spotted Ann's car in the grocery store parking lot. He'd driven by the school first. When he hadn't seen her car there and she hadn't been at home, he went cruising through town.

He parked, slid out of the truck and went around to the passenger side to get Bets. If he couldn't get Ann to come home because she was going to have their baby, maybe Bets could lure her back. Desperate, Reed was ready to try anything.

He put the baby into one of the store's carts with a built-in infant seat and shoved it up and down the aisles until he spotted Ann in the meat department. To make his ploy look good, he randomly grabbed a few cans from the shelves and tossed them in the cart.

"How are you feeling?" he asked.

Her head snapped up and her radiant smile nearly curled his toes before her welcome evaporated in recognition. She gazed at him warily. "I'm fine, thank you."

"You eating okay?" His gaze slid to her stomach, which was as flat as it had ever been. He remembered the soft feel of her skin, her fading tan line where she'd worn a two-piece suit last summer, and the paler shade of milky white that had been hidden from the sun.

"Breakfasts don't sit too well, but other than that I'm doing fine."

"That's good." He stroked Bets's head and watched as Ann followed his gesture, her expression softening. "Bets has been a little cranky lately."

"Is something wrong with her?" Instinctively, she caressed Bets's cheek, her fingers brushing Reed's in the process. Bets gurgled happily and tried for a lopsided smile. Reed wanted to grab hold of Ann's hand and never let go. "Have you talked to the doctor?" she asked.

"I don't think it's anything serious. Mostly I think she misses you."

"I miss her, too." Ann's whisper was barely audible and her green eyes glistened as she looked up at Reed. "Very much."

"Then come home, sugar."

"Because of Bets?"

"I'd say she was a pretty damn good reason. Wouldn't you?"

She gave him a sad shake of her head that nearly broke his heart. "Not good enough, Reed."

His throat practically closed shut. "If not Bets, then what will bring you back?"

"Keep thinking. You'll figure it out." Turning, she shoved her cart away from him, heading down the soup aisle.

REED DIDN'T have a clue. With grim awareness, he admitted that the next afternoon as he and Jason were changing the straw in Fiero's stall.

Sure, he might be a little dense but what Ann was doing didn't make any sense. Not that he had a prayer of ever understanding a woman. She'd married him in exchange for his mentoring a snot-nosed kid who didn't have an ounce of quit in him no matter what kind of miserable job Reed tossed in his direction. Then she'd gone and paid off his loan, which he couldn't seem to get *un*paid. When he'd gotten angry about that she'd blurted out that she loved him. He hadn't believed her. He wasn't that loveable a guy.

But Ann did love Betina. He'd seen that in her eyes. Somehow Bets wasn't enough to make Ann come home.

Sure as hell, Ann must love the baby that was growing in her belly, too. She was that kind of woman.

His kid.

The thought of raising Bets had been daunting enough. Now he was going to have a kid of his own.

Masculine pride warred with the empty spot in his chest. He hadn't meant to get her pregnant. Now that she was, it was easy to picture her body thickening, her breasts growing heavy with milk.

"Are you just gonna stand there all day lookin' goofy or are we gonna get some work done?"

Reed snared Jason with a look that was meant to make his knees rattle. It didn't faze the kid. "You need to develop a little more respect for your elders."

"Yeah, sure. But I don't get paid if I don't work." He snatched the pitchfork away from Reed. "Besides, seems to me you ain't so smart if you can't get your old lady to come back."

"I tried."

"What'd you do? Yell at her like you do me?"

"No. Not that it's any of your business." So what if he had raised his voice just a little. Ann wasn't any more afraid of him than Jason was. She never backed down. *I love you,* she'd said.

"So did you tell her you love her? That's probably what she's waiting for. You know, a guy's gotta grovel.''

Reed scowled. "What makes you such an expert on women?''

Raking the straw around the stall, Jason said, "They taught us all about that in health and family living class. Women like mushy stuff.''

"Health and family living?" Reed mocked.

"Women like to be courted, see? Candy and flowers. Junk like that. It makes 'em feel special.''

Reed wasn't exactly the candy-and-flowers type. Ann would never believe him if he showed up with armloads of phony romance stuff. She was special, though. The kind of woman a man dreamed about along with home and family.

Reed had never allowed himself to have that dream.

Until Ann.

Did that mean he loved her, he wondered? He searched his conscience and came up with an answer that was stunningly simple.

Deprived of that emotion as a child, he hadn't been able to recognize it when it showed up in his life—maybe because it had sneaked up on him when he wasn't looking.

Bets had created the first opportunity for him to love someone in particular and develop a special bond. Then Ann had come along opening his heart to even newer experiences that he'd never before known. The empty place he'd been feeling in his chest since Ann left had been her missing love—the tender emotion that she'd given him and he'd flatly rejected.

No wonder she'd left him.

Reed took Jason's head between his big hands and planted a kiss right smack in the middle of the boy's sweaty forehead.

"Oh, gross. What are you doing, man?"

"You're a genius, kid."

"Yeah, I am, but—"

"And I love you."

Jason blinked and his face began to glow as if he'd just been touch by a magic wand. "Naw, nobody—"

"I do." Reed hooked the boy's head in the crook of his elbow, gently wrestling him, roughhouse style. As if the boy were his son, a cocky kid he loved.

And he loved Ann, too.

Now he knew how to get her back, a way far more special than flowers and candy.

But he'd need Dora's help from Miniature World to convince Ann and make his dream come true—a dream he'd only just realized *could* come true for someone like him.

Chapter Fifteen

Ann dusted the chalk from her fingers and turned back to the class. Her explanation of the X-Y axis hadn't generated a single spark of understanding in the glazed-over eyes of her third-period students.

"Yoohoo. Summer vacation hasn't started yet, guys. You need to get this—"

The classroom door swung open and in trotted Arnold, his tail wagging. The students immediately responded with titters and whistles. Eyes wide, her heart slamming against her breastbone, Ann's gazed remained riveted on the door. Why would Reed—

Her handsome cowboy sauntered into the room, an easy grin on his face and Bets in his arms. His boots were old and worn, his hip-hugging jeans white with wear and his Stetson rode low on his forehead. He looked sexy and wonderful—and totally out of place.

"You're disrupting my class, Reed." Her voice was breathy with surprise.

"Sorry, sugar. This is important and I'm an impatient man." He glanced around the room. "Jason, get your tail over here."

The boy scooted out of his chair. His grin was about as wide as a quarter moon.

"You know how to hold a baby without dropping her?" Reed asked.

Jason's eyes turned into saucers. "Hey, man, I'm no baby-sitter—"

"I need two hands for this," Reed said. He thrust Bets into Jason's arms, though five teenage girls shot their hands in the air begging for the honor of holding the baby. Jason staggered backward but held on to Bets. Meanwhile, Arnold was making the rounds of the students, receiving lots of pets and scratches behind his ears.

Ann rolled her eyes. She'd totally lost control of the classroom. "Reed, whatever you're up to, this isn't the right time or place."

"Sure it is." He produced a shopping bag from Dora's Miniature World and pulled out two boxes, placing them on her desk.

Bewildered by Reed's actions and worried Jason would drop the baby, Ann seated the boy at a desk where he could more safely hold Bets. When she turned, planning to physically throw Reed out of her classroom if necessary, her breath caught.

Her Dream Man miniature was in the center of her desk—a mounted cowboy with a baby in his arms and a raggedy dog at his side. She watched in amazement as he added another figure to the tiny tableau—a woman who fit right behind the handsome cowboy on his horse, her arms around his waist. She wore a bright red sweater draped around her shoulders.

Ann's vision blurred, and she covered her mouth with her hand to prevent a sob from escaping. She was the woman, the scene a magical moment from her past.

"Are you going to be sick?" Reed asked worriedly.

She shook her head. No way could she possibly speak past the constriction that had closed her throat. She could barely breathe.

The students, instead of taking advantage of the unusual situation, had gone silent as if they understood they were witnessing a momentous occasion.

Her heart overflowing with love, Ann looked up at Reed.

He took off his hat, his saddle-brown hair mashed by the band. "I never had much of a family when I was a kid. Sometimes I'd walk through town and see mothers and fathers with their children. They'd be laughing together or maybe having ice cream. I'd tell myself it didn't matter. But it did, 'cause I'd go home at night and alone in my room I'd pretend my mother was baking cookies and I was playing ball with my old man. Then he'd come home drunk as a skunk and beat the hell out of me for no good reason.

"When I had the chance to be Bets's daddy, I figured I had it pretty good. She and I could be a family, just the two of us. But I didn't know what a real family could be like until I married you. I'm so thick-headed, I couldn't see that until you left me."

A girl in the classroom sighed. Ann couldn't make even that much of a response. She was too dumbfounded by Reed's public disclosures.

"I think I've figured out a really good reason why you ought to come back home with me, sugar."

She swallowed hard. "Why, Reed?" She knew in her heart he'd found the only reason that mattered.

"I love you, Ann. I don't have a lot to offer you yet except to promise I'll work myself to the bone so we can be a family."

"All I've ever wanted is your love, Reed. That's all I'll ever need." Oblivious to their youthful audience, she opened her arms to him. "I love you, too."

Pulling her close, he covered her mouth with his. It wasn't a chaste kiss, far more intimate than she should allow under the circumstances. She didn't care. She wanted the whole world to know she loved Reed Drummond and he loved her. She'd spend the rest of her life proving it to him and anyone else who was interested.

"Hey, man, how long do I have to hold this kid? She puked all over my shirt."

The classroom erupted in laughter at Jason's dour expression. Ann realized the boy had probably been as moved as anyone in the room by Reed's revelations. He'd had a miserable childhood and hadn't yet found a way out.

"You'd better rescue Jason," she said to Reed.

"I've got a better idea," he said, glancing in the youngster's direction and winking. "Why don't we adopt him. I'd get me a hardworking ranch hand and Bets would get a big brother."

Jason's chin dropped to his chest. "You want to adopt—"

"The artist that makes these miniatures said she could add a kid to the scene any time we wanted. Assuming you're interested and the bureaucrats say it's okay."

"Well, yeah, but—" The boy scowled. "Does that mean you don't have to pay—"

The class howled at Jason's mercenary streak but Ann knew the boy wanted nothing more than to be loved—just like Reed. She supposed that's why bad boys were her one weakness.

"Do you mind?" Reed asked Ann quietly as the students continued to razz Jason. "Adopting Jason, I mean."

"I think it's a perfectly wonderful idea. And I think you're a pretty terrific man for having thought of it."

"You're the best thing that's ever happened to me. I was blind not to see from the first how much I loved you."

"But your eyes are open now."

"Hmm. And as soon as we get home, I'm gonna burn that prenuptial agreement I made you sign." He kissed her again, slowly and thoroughly. "From now on you're stuck with me, Mrs. Drummond. I'm never going to stop loving you."

That was fine by Ann. She'd found her own life-size dream man, a rogue cowboy, and never planned to let him go. And she didn't plan to keep him on the mantel either, she thought with a secret grin, but right next to her in a bed plenty big enough for two.

Look for a new and exciting series from Harlequin!

*Two **new** full-length novels in one book, from some of your favorite authors!*

Starting in May, each month we'll be bringing you two new books, each book containing two brand-new stories about the lighter side of love! Double the pleasure, double the romance, for less than the cost of two regular romance titles!

Look for these two new Harlequin Duets™ titles in May 1999:

Book 1:
WITH A STETSON AND A SMILE
by Vicki Lewis Thompson
THE BRIDESMAID'S BET
by Christie Ridgway

Book 2:
KIDNAPPED? by Jacqueline Diamond
I GOT YOU, BABE by Bonnie Tucker

2 GREAT STORIES BY 2 GREAT AUTHORS FOR 1 LOW PRICE!

Don't miss it! Available May 1999 at your favorite retail outlet.

HARLEQUIN®
Makes any time special.™

Look us up on-line at: http://www.romance.net

HDGENR